The Romance Report

Amy E. Lilly

The characters in this book are fictitious or are referred to in a fictional context. Any similarity to real persons, living or dead, is coincidental.

Library of Congress Control Number: 2015914169

1st Edition

Bella Lilly Press
Spanishburg, WV

Cover Art by Shari Lilly Flynn.

ISBN-13: 9780692515457

DEDICATION

For Maricruz and Laurie. They tolerate me.

PHEE JEFFERSON SERIES

DEATH IS LONG OVERDUE
SUMMER READING IS KILLING ME
PERMANENTLY DELETED (DECEMBER 2015)

STAND ALONE TITLES

THE ROMANCE REPORT

ACKNOWLEDGMENTS

My eternal gratitude to my friends and family for their support and ability to ignore me when I get crabby due to writer's block. I couldn't have done this without Maricruz Baker and her mother, Ophelia. Her late night phone calls of encouragement and her mother's research and input helped make this book possible. And to the inspiration for Quinn, Elizabeth L. One day she'll know how much value she has.

CHAPTER ONE

Quinn struggled to buckle her 3-inch black Prada heels while holding her cell phone between her shoulder and ear. "I can't say no to my mother. She's a force of nature when it comes to running my life. Right shoes, right career, right guy. She's making up for all of those years that she and Dad were on the road."

"It's a bad idea to take a date with you to review a restaurant," Indie said. "I would have told her you had a meeting with your boss or something."

Quinn's phone beeped indicating another call. She looked at the screen. "I swear that woman knows when I'm talking about her. I've got to go, Indie. It's Mom."

"Call me and let me know how the date goes."

Quinn clicked over and answered, "Hello, Mom. Yes, I'm wearing the dress you bought me for my birthday."

"How did you know I was going to ask? Black is slimming, dear."

Quinn hopped around some more trying to buckle the other shoe. In frustration, she tossed the phone on her unmade bed. Her mother's voice continued its lecture oblivious to the fact that Quinn wasn't listening. She buckled the straps and slipped the black dress from its hanger and over her head. Quinn picked up the phone. "As I was saying, your father and I don't understand why you insisted on taking the job with this half-baked website. We have contacts and could get you a real job."

"It is a real job with a real magazine, Mom. The world is changing. Publishers are moving to the digital world. I read your articles online with my morning coffee. It's great not traipsing out at six a.m. to get the morning edition. I boot up my laptop and there you are."

"What's the name of this magazine again?"

"It's called Under the Radar. Randall Kent, the owner, wants to feature restaurants, clubs and shops that don't get reviewed but should. Tonight I'm checking out an Italian fusion restaurant called

Marlowe's," Quinn said.

"It's in poor taste to mix work and dating, but tonight was the only night Tad had free while he's in the city. He's on target to make partner at the same law firm as his father. You remember T.K., dear. Your father went on that yearly deep sea fishing trip with him and a few others. Good family."

"Yes, Mother." Quinn answered on autopilot. She wondered if her mom realized the only time Quinn called her Mother was when she lectured Quinn like she was still twelve. "I promise I'll behave and not embarrass you. I'm sure Tad mixes business with pleasure, too. Isn't that what corporate lawyers do? Seal the deal over a cocktail and perhaps a pole dancer or two?"

"Don't be crude. I'll talk to you tomorrow," Anne Daniels said curtly and hung up.

Quinn sighed again. Open mouth and insert a Prada heel. It seemed to happen more and more these days whenever she talked to her parents. Both worked as reporters for a national newspaper. Her dad focused on the political scene while her mother wrote about world events. When she was young, they were gone all of the time. Now that they were well established in their careers, they were able to stay home more often. Quinn knew they both expected her to follow in their footsteps and work for a big newspaper. They didn't understand that after she finished her degree and got a job at the local paper, she felt lost. Her three months traveling abroad with Uncle Patrick should have shaken her out of her funk. Instead, a lingering sense of restlessness remained.

She finished applying her makeup and brushed her long, dark hair into a severe ponytail. She added a deep rouge lip stain that made her pale complexion even paler. "I might not be a fashion model, but I wouldn't toss me out with yesterday's fish," Quinn told her reflection then blew herself a kiss.

She checked the time on her cell phone. If she didn't hustle, she'd be late to meet Tad. She grabbed her purse and keys and headed out the door. As she clattered down the stairs from her apartment, she rounded the corner and slammed right into a solid wall. A solid wall with muscles and a hint of men's cologne that wore a suit and tie. Her eyes moved upward, and Quinn saw an amused smile on the face in front of her. An attractive man with sandy brown hair and a hint of a five o'clock shadow on his chin looked down at her. He held a leather duffel bag in one hand.

"I'm so sorry," Quinn apologized. "I was in a hurry to meet someone and wasn't watching where I was going."

"I'm sure I'll survive the assault. I'm Zach Taylor. I moved in last week. You must be Quinn. I meant to come introduce myself before now, but fate has intervened and saved me from bad manners." Zach held out his hand. Quinn grasped it. Unlike some men, his handshake was firm without crushing her fingers. The worst kind of handshake was the limp and clammy one.

"It's nice to meet you. I hate to be rude, but I'm already late for a date," Quinn blurted out.

"I'd hate to keep the lucky guy waiting. Stop by for coffee and a chat anytime. It's been a pleasure meeting you," Zach said.

"You, too. And again, I'm really sorry for barreling into you. Bye!" Quinn gave a quick wave with her hand and headed down the next flight of stairs.

Exiting her brownstone, she looked around for a cab. Not spotting one, she strode down the sidewalk towards downtown. After two blocks at a breakneck pace, Quinn's feet already ached. The heels she wore might be smoking hot, but they were torture devices as far as she was concerned. She'd rather wear a pair of flip flops than heels of this height. Marlowe's was at least ten more blocks away. Thank goodness she spotted a cab letting off a fare. She whistled and hobbled her way down the sidewalk to grab it. A few blissful minutes off her feet later, the cab delivered her to the restaurant.

Quinn spotted Tad Kincaid at a table in the far corner of the restaurant, and waving away the hostess, she made her way to the table. "Sorry I'm late, Tad. I ran into my new neighbor as I headed out the door."

"I was thinking you had stood me up. There's a first time for everything," Tad said. He reached up a hand and smoothed his blonde hair. Quinn hadn't seen him since he was a teenager. He had changed little in the intervening years. He still sported the same clean-cut, All-American male looks he did when he was seventeen. She wondered if his ego was the same as well.

"I'm sorry," Quinn said again as she sat down across from him. She longed to take off the offending heels. Her feet felt like two giant sweet potatoes fresh out of a hot oven. She needed to loosen the straps before they exploded out of the Prada shoes. "It's been a long time. You look good."

"Thanks." Tad preened. He leaned forward and whispered, "What's the deal with this restaurant? The chef came out a little while ago and I swear he looked like he got released from a prison chain gang. He had more tattoos and piercings than a biker. If you want to go somewhere else, we can."

Quinn reached down and tried to unfasten the buckle on her shoes. "Todd Marlowe is supposed to be the up and coming chef in Italian fusion food. He's edgy and modern. He went to a top cooking school in Paris, not Prison Cooking 101 class. I'm sure it'll be fine." She pretended to get something from her purse. She grabbed the offending buckle, yanked it open and eased her foot out of the shoe. Quinn glanced down and saw Tad was wearing a pair of Gucci loafers. Without socks. Not even no show socks from what she could tell. Appalled by the imagined stench of his leather bound sweaty feet, she accidentally banged her head on the table as she hurried to rid herself of the image of Tad's toes. "Ouch!"

"Are you okay?" Tad said with what seemed more like annoyance than concern.

"I'm fine. I was trying to turn my cell phone off so it wouldn't disturb us," Quinn lied.

"Good. There's nothing I hate more than someone talking nonstop on their phone during dinner. I'm an attorney. My clients need constant access to me, but I draw the line at having the phone on at dinner," Tad said with a self-important tone. "So, Quinn, what have you been doing since the last time I saw you…what was it? Ten years ago?"

"Just about. If I recall correctly, it was your brother Rodney's sixteenth birthday party. You were home from university and didn't have time for silly teenagers."

"Well," Tad chuckled, "you know what it's like with little brothers and sisters. They're annoying until they finish puberty."

"Not really," Quinn said. She guessed Tad forgot she was an only child. The waiter arrived and handed them menus.

"My name is Jack and I'll be your waiter this evening. Our special is a Shrimp Fra Diavolo. It's jumbo shrimp served in a spicy marinara sauce and garnished with mussels, clams and basil. Would you like to see our wine list?"

"Yes," Quinn started.

"No, that's unnecessary. We'd like a glass of your house red to start, and I'll take prime rib, rare, with a baked potato and green beans."

"Sir, we don't serve prime rib," Jack said, confusion on his face.

"You don't serve prime rib? Really? Quinn, your mother said you reviewed high-end restaurants online. What four-star restaurant doesn't serve prime rib?"

"This is an Italian fusion restaurant. It's Italian with a Caribbean flair, not English," Quinn explained. "And I try not to let the restaurant realize I'm writing about their food. It screws the pooch if you do."

Tad's face twisted in consternation as he absorbed what Quinn said. "Hmmm…I'm not familiar with Italian fusion food, but what the heck, I'm nothing if not open-minded. Jack, give us a few minutes and get back to us. In the meantime, if you could bring us the house red, that'd be great."

"Jack, one moment. Could you bring me a glass of Chardonnay, please? House is fine, but a glass of water with a twist of lemon to go with it would be outstanding."

"Certainly. I'll be right back." Jack almost saluted as he turned and hurried away from what was turning into a tense evening.

Quinn looked over the top of her menu at Tad. He was exactly the kind of guy her mom would adore. Clean-cut, well-educated, and a good job. A solid middle-class male. She could even see the start of a receding hairline. Tad would be bald as his dad by forty. He was probably boring as hell, too. His father, T.K., was. Quinn shook her head. She had promised her mother she would give Tad a chance. After her last boyfriend disaster, anything would be an improvement. Thomas, the hot guitarist, turned out to be a little too hot for her to handle. Actually, the items in his apartment were hot. Quinn considered herself lucky that he'd only "borrowed" her bedroom television and not everything she owned. She shook her head as she remembered his telephone call asking her for bail money. No more artists or musicians, Quinn promised herself. From now on she planned to date nice, normal men with boring day jobs.

"Earth to Quinn. Hello? Is anyone home?"

Quinn realized Tad had been speaking to her. "I'm sorry," Quinn apologized for what seemed like the hundredth time that day. "I'm trying to decide what to order. Everything looks so good."

"I'll stick with the seafood fettucine. Half the stuff on the menu doesn't even sound like food. I'm a meat and potatoes guy with a little pasta now and then. I'm made in America. I like American food. Nothing weird like octopus or snails for this guy. I run and lift weights three days a week. I like to load on the carbs before a run, but give me a juicy rib eye and I'm fat, dumb and happy," Tad said.

"Wow. I'm impressed. You're in great shape." Quinn threw the proverbial dog a bone. See, Mother, I can flirt with the best of them.

"Yep. Sitting behind a desk all day isn't good for the old arteries even at my age. Besides, love the old man, but his spare tire is not something I plan to inherit." Tad patted his flat stomach. He made sure to lean forward and subtly flex his chest muscles. Quinn tried not to grimace.

Jack returned with the glasses of wine and Quinn's water. "I hope you'll find our house wines to your liking. The owner takes particular pride in stocking the wine cellar with outstanding vintages. Our house wines come from a small winery in the Virginia Piedmont."

Quinn sipped her wine and nodded in appreciation. "It's wonderful. Just the right amount of oak with a hint of smokiness."

"Not bad. Jack, I'd like the seafood fettucine. Quinn?"

"I'll be adventurous tonight. I'd like the wild boar *asado* with sour orange mojo. I love plantains and can't wait to try this dish."

"Superb choice, madam. May I suggest a Grenache with your meal. It pairs well with the wild boar," Jack said. "We have one from Pasado Vineyards I guarantee you will love."

"Sounds great. I'll trust your judgment."

"Excellent." Jack took their menus and headed towards the kitchen.

"You realize that they suggest those wines to up sell you. I guarantee you the wine he suggested is one of the more expensive wines on the list," Tad informed her.

Quinn bit back the urge to call Tad a tight wadded twit. She picked up her glass of wine and took her time sipping it. "Don't worry," she said, her voice sticky with saccharine sweetness, "it's on my expense account. This is a business dinner, not a date."

Tad let out an annoyed huff. "I can afford any wine this place serves. I was trying to be helpful. I waited tables at a swanky restaurant during undergrad. Dad thought it would build character for me to earn my spending money."

"Writing about food and wine is how I make my bread and butter," Quinn replied, feeling guilty for not being nicer to Tad. Maybe he was trying to be helpful. Lots of people didn't know about the restaurant business or wine. Perhaps he wasn't the jerk he used to be. She blamed the sockless loafers. They screamed spoiled son of the country club set. She wondered how the leather didn't shrink from the sweaty feet. "Plus, I spent three months touring the restaurants of Italy and Spain with my uncle who's a chef."

"That's right. I forgot about your uncle. Dad was telling me he owned a little diner that received some positive press."

"It's a restaurant, not a diner, and yes, it's received rave reviews. Uncle Patrick is putting a new flair on Irish fare. It's not mutton and potatoes anymore. He's going to the local farms and incorporating fresh produce and meat into new dishes. Anyway, he and I traveled to out of the way eateries and met several amazing chefs and home cooks. His plan is to incorporate what he learned and create something different from other restaurants. I'm excited."

"At least you can cook. I'm all thumbs in the kitchen. You must fix me a home-cooked meal soon."

Fortunately Quinn was saved from responding to Tad's not so subtle hint by the arrival of dinner. Jack slid her plate in front of her. She swooned from the intoxicating scent of oranges mixed with spices. She closed her eyes and inhaled. When she opened them a few moments later, she saw Tad holding a forkful of food in front of his face and peering closely at it.

"I don't think this is seafood fettucine," he said.

"Why do you say that? It looks like it to me."

"No. It smells funny." He sniffed and wrinkled his nose. "This," he shoved the offending fork at Quinn, "has some kind of weird spice or something besides seafood and pasta."

Quinn looked at the forkful of pasta. She reached over and took it from him. She tried a bite and tasted nothing out of the ordinary. "It's fine. Try it. If you'd prefer, we can trade dishes."

"I don't want your dinner," Tad said each word slowly as if she didn't understand English. "What I want is a freakin' prime rib and a normal dinner. Instead, I get some weird fusion pasta crap and crabs." Tad slammed the fork down on the table. His hand hit the edge of his pasta plate on its downward journey. The plate flipped, and the pasta flew across the table and landed all over Quinn.

All conversation in the restaurant stopped. Quinn felt a noodle slide off her head and down into her cleavage. A shrimp somersaulted off the edge of the table and into one of her Prada heels.

"What is wrong with you?" Quinn said through gritted teeth. "You are a pompous, spoiled brat. I can't believe my mother thought we'd hit it off. I'd rather date a rabid raccoon than you!" She spotted Jack easing his way towards their table, unsure if it was a smart move or a death wish. She reached down and dumped the errant shrimp from her shoe.

"I'm a spoiled brat?" Tad hooted. "Really? I took you out as a favor to your parents. It's not like I make a habit of dating flaky chicks in dead-end jobs. You're lucky I even bothered to show up. I turned down a date with a gorgeous accountant to go out with you, a loser who writes a blog about food." He threw a hundred dollar bill on the table and stood up to leave.

Quinn felt the blood rushing to her face. A hot anger roiled up from her stomach. "What the hell kind of name is Tad? It's a frog, for Pete's sake, not a name for a grown-ass man. And it's an online magazine, not a blog!" Quinn yelled. She picked up one of her shoes and threw it at Tad. Time slowed as it sailed through the air, toe over heel. It sailed right past Tad and hit smack dab into the head of the gentleman sitting behind him.

CHAPTER TWO

To: Randall Kent

From: Quinn Daniels

Subject: Change in Restaurant Review

Randall,

Due to unforeseen circumstances, I was unable to review Marlowe's Restaurant. I apologize for the delay. I plan to review Gryphon's this evening and I will have the review in your inbox for approval by 8 a.m. Friday morning. Again, I apologize for the delay.

Quinn

To: Quinn Daniels

From: Randall Kent

Subject: Re: Change in Restaurant Review

Quinn,

Let's talk about this. Come see me in my office today at 2 p.m.

Randall

Quinn strolled through the glass door announcing in discreet black letters Kent Publications, Inc. at a few minutes before 2 p.m. Ginger, the chic brunette who manned the front desk and guarded Randall Kent's office like Quinn's cat guarded her toy mouse, was talking on the phone. Ginger wiggled her French-tipped fingers to Quinn and mouthed, "Go on in."

Quinn stuck her head into Randall's office. Randall sat frowning at his laptop. He looked up, scowled and motioned for her to have a seat.

"So, Randall, I'm sorry about dropping the ball on the Marlowe's review. Something came up and honestly, is Italian-Caribbean fusion a trend we want to promote? It might appear like we're jumping on whatever food trend is hot for the moment, but if it lasts less than six months, it lessens our credibility. A review of Gryphon's would be a better tie-in to the entertainment piece that Brian's writing about the remodeled theater on the same block," Quinn said hurriedly. "I promise you I can review Gryphon's and have the article to you by tomorrow morning."

"Something came up? Would you care to elaborate on what that might have been? Say perhaps an arrest for disturbing the peace, simple assault, destruction of property…this is according to my contacts in the police department. Shall I continue?" Randall asked in a tight voice. He leaned back in his chair, crossed his arms and fixed Quinn with a glare.

Quinn gulped. She wouldn't finagle herself out of this one. She came clean. "My mother insisted I go on a date with the son of a family friend. He was a complete ass and threw pasta all over me. I lost my temper. I didn't mean to bean the guy in the head with my shoe. It was an accident."

"An accident is spilling a glass of wine. An accident is hitting the rear end of the car in front of you. An accident is not picking up a shoe and assaulting someone in the middle of a crowded restaurant and having a video of it blasted across social media!" Randall's rose in volume until the glass shook in the window behind him.

"Wait," Quinn said, "there's a video?"

"Yes!" Randall snarled and spun his laptop around for her. "A couple was celebrating their twenty-fifth wedding anniversary last night. Their kids were shooting video with their phones of their dad giving his wife an anniversary band. Imagine how thrilled they were to capture you screaming like a banshee with a shrimp hanging off your ear in the background." He punched a key with his finger and the video played.

Quinn felt her stomach sink into her ankles. She should have stood up to her mother and said no to the date with Tad. She watched in horror as the events of the previous evening played on the screen. The budding filmmakers had even gone so far as to add special effects to the final scene. Quinn's Prada heel bounced repeatedly off the bald head of the man with the comic book style "Kapow!" emblazoned on the screen with each ricochet.

"Crap," Quinn said in a small voice. She sank down in her chair.

"Crap is right. A heap of crap is what you've tossed my good name in with your behavior. Not only did I get an angry phone call from Todd Marlowe demanding Under the Radar write a public apology and a glowing review, but the man you hit with the shoe is none other than the brother of the mayor. Fortunately for you, he decided not to press charges. I also managed to convince the police to drop the matter. Unfortunately for you, you're out of a job and a career because I'll be damned if I give you a reference. I don't care if your uncle is the chef to the president himself, you're finished. I'm not going to have my magazine's reputation smeared by the juvenile antics of a self-indulged spoiled brat throwing a temper tantrum. Now get out of my office!"

"But…" Quinn started to protest that it wasn't her fault, but the fury she saw on Randall's face stopped her cold. She slunk quietly out of his office and slipped past Ginger without a glance. It wasn't until she made her way out of the building did she allow the tears to fall. She leaned back against the cool granite and gulped in fresh air in an attempt to calm herself. Wiping her eyes, Quinn took another shuddering breath and slipped sunglasses out of her bag and put them on to hide behind the dark lenses.

"Quinnie, crying isn't going to turn that spilt milk into butter, so put your big girl panties on and get over it," Quinn said in her best imitation of her Grandma Rose's Irish brogue.

She straightened up and whistled at a passing taxi. She asked the driver to take her to her brownstone on Franklin. As the cab pulled away from the curb and whipped into the heavy traffic of Broad Street, Quinn realized this might be the last taxi she could afford in the foreseeable future. She imagined the small sum in her savings account dwindling to zero without the steady paycheck Kent Publications provided. Her small dating disaster of the night before mushroomed into a hurricane of destruction with each passing block. Rent. Utilities. Cat food for her cat, Fat Panther. People food. She needed a job and she needed one quick.

"You know what? Just drop me off here. I'll walk the rest of the way," Quinn instructed the driver. She handed him the fare and felt like a loser giving him a fifty cent tip. "Sorry about the tip. I got fired a little while ago. I can't find a decent guy and I don't know what I want to be when I grow up and…" She stifled a sob.

The driver handed her back her fare. "This rides on me, honey. I've been in some tight spots myself."

Quinn felt a fresh set of tears form at the sight of the man's friendly smile. "Thank you. I promise I'll find you once I get a job and give you the biggest tip ever."

"I'm sure you will. The name's Saul. You get in a bind, you call dispatch and ask for me. I've got a daughter about your age. I'd like to believe someone is looking out for her as she makes her way out into the world. Now get back in and let me take you the rest of the way home."

CHAPTER THREE

"The tragedy in this whole situation is a perfectly good dinner was sacrificed. Darling, if it'd been me, I'd have pulled that shrimp right out of my bustier and nibbled on it just to spite his pompous ass," Sean said. He took another sip of his cocktail. "Mmm...what did you call this thing again? It is absolutely delish."

"A Smoky Mary. It's a Bloody Mary made with smoked salt, jalapenos, and fresh tomatoes. It's my very own creation. Since I crashed and burned at my journalism gig, a smoky drink was fitting," Quinn said glumly. "I get a dream job writing about food and I blow it. I'll have to go back to working in the advertising department at the Times, if they'll even take me back. No job. No money. No man. That's it. I'm done with romance. I'm giving up on men for good. I'll become the crazy cat lady who lives in a shopping cart and eats cat chow along with her twenty feline friends.

Somebody get me a crocheted beret and unmatched socks!"

"Aren't you overreacting just a little? I mean, it was a guy your mother set you up on a date with for Pete's sake. It was bound to go sour. No offense, but your mom cares about facts, political connections and appearances. Romance is not her strong point," Indie pointed out to Quinn. She ran her small fingers through her bright blue hair causing it to spike even more. She looked like a punked-out cartoon hedgehog with glasses.

"I couldn't give up men," Sean declared as he licked the salt from the rim of his glass. He fluttered his lashes at Quinn. "This boy needs love like a flower needs sunshine. The difference between you and me is I prefer my men driving a shiny sports car with a fat …"

"Sean!" Quinn and Indie squealed in unison.

"Wallet. What? I was going to say wallet. Sheesh. Get your mind out of the gutter." He winked at them and continued, "Quinn dates poor, starving artists. Boyfriend has got to have a J O B or he is not going to date me. Standards. You've got to have standards or you'll end up homeless in a box with Johnny Nightdriver as he plays guitar for your beanie weenie supper. Now, your mama's got standards but her taste in men runs towards the kind with a stick up their…"

"Sean!" Both girls squealed again.

"Behind. Listen, I'm keeping it G-rated, but if you make me another oh-so-tasty cocktail, I can bump it up to PG-13. Anyhow, as I was saying before I was so rudely interrupted, you've got to set standards. For example, Sean Carlos' Rule Number One is boyfriend has got to have a job. Rule Number Two is he has to be smoking hot and dress to impress. Don't come pick me up in raggedy old jeans and a broken down t-shirt. You might as well pack yourself right on down the stairs and back to your shack and toothless hound dog."

"He needs to be smart," Indie chimed. "Not so smart that he's a jerk, but smart enough to be able to know what's going on in the world and talk about it."

"Funny," Quinn added. "He needs to have a sense of humor, in and out of the bedroom."

"He needs to have a big…"

"Sean!" Indie and Quinn whooped with laughter. Indie laughed so hard that she began to hiccup. Quinn patted her hard on the back in a half-hearted attempt to help. The watered-down remains of Indie's Smoky Mary spilled on the white couch.

"Crud. Sorry. Let me go grab a rag and clean it before it sets," Indie hiccupped as she attempted to stand up and make her way to the kitchen.

"Girl, that is going to stain. This is why I don't do white. Hell, this place looks like the inside of a loaf of Wonder Bread," Sean said, looking around him.

"My mother decorated. She's a firm believer that black is slimming and white furniture screams sophistication." Quinn rolled her eyes as she imagined her mother's voice in her head giving decorating advice.

"What it screams is boring. No pizazz. No personality," Sean replied.

"That's your problem," Indie said. She scrubbed at the offending red spots with a wet dishcloth. "You have no color. Everything is black and white. That works for facts and news, but life's not like that. Life is messy and colorful and…messy."

"Indie's right. You date the losers you date because you want to add a little excitement and some spark to this oh-so-drab world. You need to find a different coloring box to pick from than the one you've been choosing from lately. No more generic crayons made of cheap wax. You need the real deal," Sean announced. He stood up and strutted into Quinn's bedroom. Quinn could hear the sounds of drawers opening and shutting and hangers scraping across the metal closet rod. A few minutes later, Sean carried out a mountain of black clothing and dumped it onto the couch. "You missed your calling. You'd have gone far in life as a death metal singer or a gothic heroine in a punk rock video. Even your panties are black." Sean dangled a black thong off his pinkie finger.

"It's all become crystal clear," Indie piped. She jumped up from her seat on the ground and draped a black dress around her shoulders like a cape. "You are a vampire quietly living amongst us as you wait for your chance to swoop in and suck our blood. Mwahaha."

"Ha ha. You two are a riot. Not much I can do to change my wardrobe now. No job means no money for clothes. Remember?" Quinn got up and began to mix another batch of cocktails. She eyed the vodka bottle and added another dash of it to the pitcher in front of her. She sliced a jalapeno and garnished three glasses. "No man is ever going to want to go on a date with me once they see my screaming like a fishwife on YouTube. I might as well take my vow of celibacy now and be done with it."

Sean took the glass Quinn presented him and sipped. "Mmm…that's good. It has enough kick to put my creative juice into overdrive. Shawna, the most sought after queen in the city, is gonna give you a makeover. By the time I'm done with you, no one will recognize you, not even your mama."

"I'm not sure about you giving me a makeover, Sean. I don't do the heavy eyeliner and flashy sequins thing," Quinn protested. She imagined herself with Tammy Faye eyelashes and platform heels tottering into a five-star restaurant.

"Puhlease!" Sean waved his hand at her. "Like you could carry that style. No. I've got a friend whose mother is a buyer for some big department store. She gets tons of clothes and doesn't even wear half of it. She's begging me to take it and give it to some of the other girls in the business. Carrie is about your size so most of it should fit. In the meantime, let's do something about your hair."

"What's wrong with my hair?"

"It's black," Indie said. She had settled her tiny frame cross-legged on top of the pile of black clothes.

"I am not dyeing my hair blue or purple or green."

"What's your natural hair color?" Indie asked. "I've known you for ten years and have no clue."

"What makes you think it's not black?" Indie raised one skeptical eyebrow at Quinn. "Alright. It's boring brown."

"Give me a minute to grab some supplies from downstairs, and I'll turn you into a goddess of love."

Sean went out the door of Quinn's apartment to the ground floor where he lived with his grandmother. His grandmother, Reyna Garza, owned the building and had lived in the brownstone since she married in the late 1950s. Her husband had passed away fifteen years ago, but until recently, she was able to manage on her own. A fall down the icy front steps last winter had prompted Sean to give up his apartment in the Fan

District and move in to care for her while she recovered from a broken ankle. His grandmother didn't know about Sean's other persona, Shawna, and he had no intention of telling her. She believed Sean worked as a bouncer in a nightclub. The truth was that Sean aka Shawna headlined at Hello Sailor! Nightclub in downtown Richmond three nights a week. Under the smoky lights of the club, Sean transformed from a handsome young Latino to a raven-haired minx with a sultry voice belting out 1940s wartime ballads.

"Do not let him turn me into Dolly Parton," Quinn begged Indie. She took a big gulp of her drink and gasped as the heat of the jalapeno mixed with the vodka washed down her throat. "I still want to be me after he's done." A fine sheen of sweat broke out on her brow. She wasn't sure if it was from the jalapeno or the fear of the pending makeover.

"Do you even know who the real you is?" Indie asked. "I'm serious. It seems like everything you do is tied to your mother's approval. Your degree, your décor, even your wardrobe. Your only act of rebellion was quitting your job at the paper and taking off to Europe with your uncle. What happened to that girl?"

"I don't know," Quinn said in a small voice. "Grandma Rose went into the nursing home and living at home with my parents wasn't an option if I wanted to keep my sanity. I think Mom and Dad were gone for work so much that I want a way to connect with them. Besides, I'm twenty-six years old. Jetting off to Europe was fun, but I have to have a job and an apartment. I have to be a grown up."

"Grown up doesn't mean giving up who you are, Quinn," Indie said gently.

"Ladies, I've come armed and dangerous," Sean burst into the apartment toting to round cases festooned with 1950's pinups. "Have comb and will travel for any hair emergency!"

Quinn held her empty glass out to Indie. "Fill her up. I'm going to need it."

Quinn leaned her head over her kitchen sink and allowed Sean to rinse the strange goo he'd smeared all over her hair. She was scared to even ask him why it was purple and smelled like hardboiled eggs and ammonia. She said a silent prayer to the god of good hair to please not let her hair fall out and leave her bald as a buzzard egg.

"Okay. It's done. Your color looks fabulous if I do say so myself. Why you covered up these gorgeous chestnut locks with shoeshine black is beyond me," Sean said as he inspected her hair. He guided Quinn to a chair he'd put on the small balcony. "Now for the cut."

Quinn clutched the damp towel wrapped around her head. "Cut!" She squawked. "No one said anything about cutting my hair. I don't like short hair!"

"Hey!" Indie protested. "I just shake and roll my way out the door. Short hair is great." She shook her blue spikes at Quinn.

"Yes, but you are four foot nothing. Short hair makes you look cute. On me, I'd look like a man. Mom says I have strong features. Long hair feminizes my face," Quinn informed her. She clutched the towel even tighter as Sean attempted to pull it free.

"Like your mother knows hair. She has the same Hilary bob she got in 1995." Sean rolled his eyes. "I'm not going to cut it short. Trust me. I have more fashion sense in my little finger than most people have in their entire body."

Quinn relented and released her death grip

on the towel. Sean threw it to the side and took a sip of his drink while he inspected Quinn's face. His nose scrunched and he let out small grunts as he circled her chair. He checked her over one last time, picked up his shears and began to snip her hair. Quinn gasped as she saw long strands of hair fall to the floor around her. She closed her eyes and muttered under her breath.

"What's that? I can't hear you," Sean said. "Relax. You're going to be my greatest masterpiece. The Mona Lisa of hair. The white whale of hairdressers everywhere. Longed for but rarely seen."

"Oh brother," Indie groaned from inside the apartment. "Your ego is growing with every snip. How did you become such a diva?"

"My brother took all my testosterone in the womb," Sean said.

"Wait. You have a brother? How come I haven't met him?" Quinn asked.

"Julian is my twin brother and he's in the military. He's as straight and macho as I'm gay and fabulous. He does something with helicopters and weapons. I don't know. Stuff that gets you muddy." Sean waved his scissors in the air. "You'll meet him soon enough and love him. All the ladies do and he loves them back."

"Once you're done with her hair, I'm going to snap a picture to post on her profile page," Indie said.

"What profile page?" Quinn eyes flew open. She wanted to see what Indie was doing and why she needed a picture of her.

"The profile page I'm creating on True Hearts. I do some freelance computer security for them and occasionally tweak the algorithms they use to match prospective dates. I'm making you your very own account and thanks to my mad skills creating backdoors into their server, its free," Indie said. Her fingers flew across the keys of her laptop. She gave one last tap to the keyboard then set it on the table. She walked out onto the balcony to inspect Sean's work. "Wow! I take back everything I was thinking about your big head. Quinn, you're stunning!"

"Your undying adoration is apology enough. No peeking, Quinn. I want to tame those Neanderthal eyebrows of yours, and then we'll do the big reveal," Sean said. He pulled tweezers out and began to pluck.

"Ouch!" Quinn squirmed as Sean continued to pluck away at her brows. "This is why I don't wax or tweeze my brows. It hurts! I thought the natural brow was the newest trend."

"Natural, yes. Unruly, no. The price of traffic-stopping beauty, my love, does not come without a little pain and plucking. Quit bitching and hold still. If you're not careful you'll end up with a uni-brow on one side."

Quinn winced but forced herself to sit still. "Online dating is such a bad idea. A couple friends of mine tried it. The guys they met were nothing like their profiles. What if my date ends up being some kind of psychopathic killer? You might find me chopped into little bits and buried in the backyard."

"Which is why I set up your profile on True Hearts. They run background checks and charge big bucks for their services. It tends to cut out the creeps and cheapskates. Just try it. You might find your true love through True Hearts and record a testimonial for their commercials! You need a job. It could be extra cash!"

"Ugh. No thank you. One date and that's all. I should swear off men for life anyway. My luck with men has been depressing," Quinn said.

Sean gave a grunt of annoyance. "All this jibber jabber is messing up my genius and making her face move. Zip it!"

A few minutes later, Sean set the tweezers aside and sighed. "My masterpiece is done. You can safely go back to Marlowe's because no one will recognize you."

Quinn opened her eyes and looked in the mirror Sean held in his hand. Her black locks were transformed into natural chestnut brown waves that curled around her face making it appear slimmer. Her silver-gray eyes seemed larger now that her brows had been plucked into submission. She turned her head to get a better look at the haircut. She had to admit that Sean did amazing work. Her hair was shorter, but still waved down to her shoulders so she could pull it up into a ponytail. "I love it," she admitted. She let out a small whoop of happiness and stood up. "I'm bringing hotness back…don't worry baby, I don't wear no black…" Quinn sang and danced her way into the kitchen to refill her glass. "Now about this apartment…"

CHAPTER FOUR

"I can't believe your grandmother kept all this," Indie said as she burrowed further into the pile of boxes stacked in a dusty corner of the basement. A small sneeze erupted from her as she emerged holding a brightly colored mask. "This stuff is really cool. Kind of 1950s kitsch mixed with a Mexican flair."

"My *abuelo* was a pack rat. He kept everything left behind by the previous owners and the collection grew after each old tenant moved," Sean explained. He held up a bright blue lampshade. "This would look amazing in your place, Quinn."

"You think?" Quinn held up a black and white framed photograph of the Eiffel Tower. "I kind of like this."

Sean snatched the picture out of her hands. "We're trying to brighten your décor, not add to the current zebra color scheme. Remember?"

"What if we put it in this awesome picture frame I found? Groovy baby!" Indie emerged with a bright red frame and wore a pair of round blue-shaded sunglasses circa John Lennon.

"Doable," Quinn said. "Let's throw a couple of things in a box and take it upstairs. I don't want to go into color overload so early in my transformation."

"Definitely need this retro afghan." Sean held up a chevron-patterned throw in shades of red, blue, green and yellow. "It's like a sarape on caffeine."

Indie put the picture frame and a poster of Jerry Garcia in the box. "The poster's for me," she explained. Although the Sixties Revolution had missed them by a few years, Alison and Greg Skye managed to find a commune in rural Virginia that survived the onslaught of the eighties. Indie teethed on bean sprouts and homemade, chemical free cookies made from crunchy, good-for-you ingredients. It wasn't until her rebellious teenage years that she made her stand and demanded the chance to go to public school. She wanted to see how other teenagers lived. Her parents were firm believers that children should be allowed to choose for themselves. They acquiesced, and Indie discovered her true love in the form of a beat up high school computer. By the time she was twenty-one and graduating from college, she was a veritable computer genius and world-class hacker.

"Missed that bullet," Quinn mumbled to herself.

"What? You're kidding me, right? My parents are big time Deadheads. Jerry Garcia was a genius," Indie protested.

"I'm staying out of this catfight," Sean said. He added the blue lampshade and a silver-toned lamp to the box. "Carry the afghan, Quinn, and we'll head back up to start Operation Quinnover."

"Quinnover? I need to mix better drinks if that's the best you can come up with. How about Operation Quinntastic or Quinn 2.0?" Quinn grabbed the blanket and started up the stairs.

"I vote for Quinn 2.0," Indie piped. She grabbed up a lava lamp and an old denim rag rug she'd rescued from the basement and followed Quinn.

"Or Quinnielicious?" Quinn said over her shoulder. Quinn rounded the corner and ran straight into her new neighbor Zach.

"If I realized that a beautiful woman running into my arms every day was included in the rent, I would have moved in here years ago," Zach chuckled. He grasped Quinn's shoulders to steady her.

"I'm so sorry!" Quinn felt the blood rush straight from her boots to her roots. "I, uh, was busy talking to my friends and wasn't watching where I was going."

Sean stepped forward and held out his hand. "I'm Sean Carlos. You and I met the other day when you came to get the keys to the apartment."

"I remember. Mrs. Garza is your grandmother. Nice lady," Zach said, shaking Sean's hand. "Can I help carry anything? Is someone moving in?" He lifted an inquiring eyebrow at Quinn and then looked at Indie.

"No. We're doing a little redecorating. Zach, this is my friend, Indie. Indie, my new neighbor, Zach Taylor."

"If you're not doing anything, you should come help us redecorate Quinn's apartment," Sean suggested. "We are in the midst of Operation Quinn 2.0. We could use an impartial opinion."

"Operation Quinn 2.0?" Zach gave Sean a

quizzical look.

"Quinn is in desperate need of a boost to her love life and career. Her nearest and dearest friends, Indie and yours truly, are helping her out."

Quinn prayed that the stairs beneath her would collapse and plummet her back into the basement and away from where she stood. She glared at Sean, but he yammered on as he led Zach up the final flight of stairs to Quinn's apartment. "Quinn's adding some color to her apartment. It might inspire her to perk up her love life."

"I see," Zach said slowly as he looked around the apartment. "The place could definitely use a little brightening up. It's…what's the word?"

"Boring?" Indie volunteered.

"Austere," Zach said diplomatically. "Is the new hairdo part of Quinn 2.0? If so, I like it."

"Thanks," Quinn ducked her head and tucked a strand of her hair behind her ear. "Can I get you something to drink? Kicking Mule? Smoky Mary?"

"Are those drinks or gang names for your friends here?" Zach jerked a thumb at Sean and Indie who both plopped down on the couch.

"Drinks. If you like tomatoes and jalapenos,

you should try my Smoky Mary."

"Sure. I need a break from unpacking anyway."

"So, Zach, are you single?" Sean asked. Quinn shot daggers from the kitchen. Sean gave her his best "who me?" innocent look.

"I am currently between relationships," Zach said with a grin. "I've got too much on my plate with work and the move to date right now."

"Too bad. I was hoping I could persuade you to fix Quinn's disastrous love life," Sean said.

Quinn cleared her throat. She glared at Sean and made a slashing motion against her throat with her hand.

"I apologize for my friend, Sean. He's in love with love and thinks everyone needs a man in their life," Indie explained to Zach. "Quinn's had a run of bad luck in the love department. Her career is pretty much tanked, too. However, thanks to my mad computer skills and Sean's talent for bedazzling, her luck is about to change."

"Seriously, guys? Please tell a stranger my whole life story. Zach, you're going to need a double if you hang around these two." Quinn handed Zach his drink.

"It's okay. I have two younger sisters who both got married this year. They're constantly trying to set me up with their single friends. I don't have any plans to walk down the aisle in the near future and it's making them crazy. Me telling them that the right woman hasn't come along just adds fuel to their fire. Tell me something, Quinn. I'm curious to know why you're cursed. Did you break a mirror or walk under a ladder?" Zach joked. He took a sip of his drink.

"I'm not cursed. I went on a date with a jerk and ended up getting fired because of it," Quinn replied.

"The guy she dated before that plays guitar on a street corner for spare change and stole from her," Sean said.

"And the guy she dated before that is going to end up on America's Most Wanted one day," India chimed in. She shot Quinn an apologetic look. "It's true. He was sketchy."

"Maybe you should give up on dating," Zach said with a smile. "Either that or get someone to remove the curse you're under."

"OMG! That's it! I'm taking you to the *curandera*. Someone's cursed you!" Sean exclaimed then made the sign of the cross.

"Really? I don't need a healer to uncurse me or whatever you call it. I simply need to stay away from anything with a penis and find a job."

"You might not believe in them, but trust me when I say that a *curandera* can take care of both those problems without batting an eyelash," Sean said.

"I'll think I'll leave before the man bashing begins." Zach set his empty glass on the coffee table in front of him and stood up. "It was nice meeting you. Quinn, I still owe you that coffee. No strings attached."

Quinn walked him to her apartment door. "Listen. I'm sorry my friends were a little pushy. They mean well, but sometimes they get a little carried away with their joking."

"No problem. I have a few buddies like them. They're looking out for you. It's not a bad thing. I better get back to unpacking. See you later."

Quinn closed the door behind him. "I can't believe you two pouncing on the new neighbor and trying to set him up with me!"

"I know, right? He is much too nice and employed for you," Sean said with a snarky grin.

"I'm going to go ask the guy digging through the dumpster in the alley if he'd like a nice dinner and movie with a hot, young journalist. Much more your speed."

"Hey now! Any more comments like that I'll make your next drink a virgin."

"Oh, goody! I haven't had one of those since I was sixteen!"

"Ew. Instead of worrying about my love life, you need to worry about the state of my bank account. If I don't find a job, I won't be able to afford rent next month. I'll have to move in with my parents. I'd live in a box with the guy digging in the dumpster rather than listen to my mother's advice. Quinn, you shouldn't wear red. It makes you look like a raspberry. Quinn, ladies drink with a straw not from a glass. Quinn, why don't you go out with that nice investment banker who lives with his mother and probably has dead bodies buried in his basement, but he's from a good family and has potential."

"You sound just like your mom," Indie laughed. "You can always go live on the commune with my folks. They could use your help picking the veggies and making rope hammocks."

"Thanks, but no thanks. I'll start looking for a new job tomorrow. Worse comes to worst, I'll scrub toilets at the No Tell Motel. Anything is better than moving back home."

"Tonight, however, my dearest Doom and Gloom Queen, we're going to have fun. Let's bedazzle and jazz up this place. Come on, ladies, let's get our color vibe going," Sean said and stuck the blue lampshade on his head.

CHAPTER FIVE

Quinn picked up the phone to call her Uncle Patrick. It had been three weeks since she had been fired, and she still had no promising job leads.

"Quinnie Bee! How are you?" Uncle Patrick boomed. He was a large man with a shock of curly red hair. Despite having the frame of a dockworker, he moved with a grace and speed in his kitchen that always amazed Quinn.

"Hi, Uncle Pat. I'm good. Well, actually, not good. That's why I'm calling. I got fired and I desperately need a job. I'll wash dishes, wait tables, scrub toilets. Anything."

Uncle Patrick stayed silent for so long that Quinn thought she'd dropped the call. "Uncle Pat?"

"I'm here. Sorry. I was thanking my lucky stars. Do you remember Jenny, my pastry chef? She fell on her way down her apartment stairs this morning and broke her leg. She'll be out of commission for the next six weeks at least, so I need a temporary pastry chef."

"Poor Jenny! I'm not a pastry chef though," Quinn said.

"You grew up in the kitchen of my mother, the world's best baker. Don't tell me you aren't a pastry chef. You may not have gone to culinary school, but I think you'll do in a pinch. Get down here today because I've got a full house tonight."

"Alright. I'll be there in an hour. Thank you so much. I was about to call Mom and ask her if I could move back home," Quinn said.

"Heaven forbid that day should ever come. I love my sister, but Anne could make the Blessed Virgin cry with her nagging. I'll see you in an hour."

Quinn ended the call and tossed her cell phone in her purse. If she was going to make it across town in an hour, she needed to hurry. She tugged a black t-shirt over her head and slipped on a pair of dark blue jeans. Although Sean had added some bright pops of color to her wardrobe, old habits were hard to break. Looking at her reflection in the mirror, Quinn decided to add a bright red headband. I can tiptoe on the wild side with the color palette, Quinn thought. She grabbed her purse and started to head out the door when her cell phone buzzed.

"Hello?"

"Quinn, what are you doing this weekend?" Indie asked.

"Probably working. I'm helping Uncle Pat out for the next few weeks. His pastry chef fell and broke her leg."

"Crud biscuit. Have you logged on to your True Heart profile lately?"

"No. I hadn't even given it a second thought. I was serious when I said I didn't want to date."

"I thought as much, so I've been you the past few weeks. You got a heart request."

"A what?" Quinn locked her apartment door behind her and headed down the steps.

"A heart request. It's what True Hearts calls a request for a date," Indie explained. "You didn't listen to me at all when I set this up, did you? Anyway, a guy asked you for a date this weekend."

"He's a total stranger. I don't think I want to meet some guy I know nothing about for a date. I'll end up in a back alley dumpster wrapped in black plastic."

"I've been you."

"What? What do you mean?" Quinn shook her head in confusion. She walked towards the bus stop a few blocks away from her apartment to catch the next bus heading downtown.

"I've chatted online with this guy pretending to be you. His name is Paul. He's a realtor here in Richmond. If his profile picture is accurate, he's yummy."

"I don't know, Indie," Quinn said slowly. "His picture could be ten years old. He could be bald and five-hundred pounds with a wife and a little dog named Patches."

"I knew you would say that so I hacked into…forget I said that…I've checked him out and he's legit. Single, good-looking, fairly successful. Thirty-two years old. One date won't kill you."

"That's what Ted Bundy said," Quinn responded. The bus for downtown was pulling to the curb. "I've got to go. I'll go, but it will have to be a meet-up for drinks after I get off work on Saturday. Plus, you have to go with me, or I won't do it."

"Great! I'll set it up and let you know where

and when. I'll even babysit you."

"Gotta go," Quinn disconnected as she climbed onto the bus. A new job and a date. Maybe things were looking up for her.

Twenty minutes later, the bus dropped Quinn off a few blocks from Hanrahan's, her uncle's bistro. She hurried inside and spotted her uncle looking over the reservation book. "I'm here and ready to bake!" Quinn bounced up and gave him a big hug. "You've saved my bacon. I really didn't want to move back home."

"You might regret coming to work for me. I'm a harsh taskmaster when it comes to my kitchen. I expect you to be on time and bake only the best desserts. Family or no family, I'm going to have to treat you like everybody else or it'll cause problems in the back."

"I wouldn't expect anything less from the world's greatest chef," Quinn said. She was so happy to work even threats of imminent doom didn't quell her joy. "What would you like me to make for tonight's dessert choices?"

Unlike most restaurants, Hanrahan's menu varied from day to day. Uncle Patrick scoured the local markets and farms for only the freshest ingredients and based his menu on the day's finds. Although this often drove his kitchen staff to pull out their hair, he had developed a reputation for some of the finest and freshest cuisine in the city.

"I scored some fresh oysters and shrimp from one of my fishermen friends, and one of the local farms had a fresh supply of beef and lamb. I think a traditional shepherd's pie and some pasties from the lamb. I'm still thinking of what to do with my seafood and beef. Surf and turf is much too old school for Hanrahan's. Why don't you make Ma's chocolate orange Guinness cake and some bread pudding with whiskey sauce. I'll also need about seventy-five dinner rolls for tonight and some Irish soda bread. Think you can handle it?"

"Wow, that's a lot of rolls. I think I've only made twenty-five at a time before, but I've got the rest no problem."

"Jenny has the conversion chart for the rolls hanging on the wall, so that should make it easier for you."

"Great. I'll get started." Quinn followed her uncle into the back and stowed her bag in one of the small lockers for employees. She grabbed a large white apron and tied it around her waist. A quick glance at the shelves in front of her work space eased some of her jitters. Jenny was an organized baker. All the large tubs were clearly marked with ingredients. A large conversion chart with measurements for Hanrahan's breads and rolls was laminated and taped to the wall.

Quinn scrubbed her hands then chose a large metal bowl. She combined the flour, yeast, salt and water for her rolls. She plunged her hands into the bowl and began to mix the ingredients. Her hands became a sticky mess and as she continued to mix, some of her worries from the past month lifted. She gave a few final stirs with her hands, then she allowed the dough to rest for a few minutes while she washed her hands again in the large stainless steel sink. Finding a large silicone rolling mat under the counter, she laid it out and poured a small amount of olive oil onto its surface. She plopped her dough out and stretched and folded it a few times. The yeast and gluten began to work its magic and after a few tugs, it became shiny and stretchy. She smelled the warm yeast and smiled as she thought of memories from her childhood. Making bread was one of her favorite things to do with her grandmother. She missed those moments. Grandma Rose had become too fragile and ill to live at home by herself. Quinn knew that there would be no more Sundays baking with her grandmother. A small tear escaped and slid down her cheek.

"Enough of your crying, Quinnie. You've got work to do," Quinn said to herself. She covered her dough with a flour cloth and busied herself mixing the ingredients for the cake. Soon the whole kitchen filled with the scent of rising bread and warm chocolate.

"Mmmm…smells marvelous in here," Uncle Patrick commented when he came to check on her progress a few hours later. He seemed pleased with the rows of piping hot rolls with their lightly browned crusts. Picking one up, he tore a chunk off and popped into his mouth. "Don't tell Ma, but I swear your bread is just a wee bit better than hers."

"Thanks," Quinn said, pleased. She blew a stray hair away from her face and wiped her floured hands on the front of her apron. "Everything is done and ready for tonight."

"Fantastic. You can head home and I'll see you tomorrow morning. I'd like to have you in here by no later than eight o'clock every morning so you're done before the rest of the crew arrives and takes over the kitchen. I was lucky you were able to come in and save the day this afternoon, but I hate to cut it so close to the dinner hour."

"I'll be here," Quinn said as she removed her apron and tossed it into the hamper near her locker. She hugged her uncle again. "Thanks again for giving me a job, even for the short term. It will hold me over until I can find something else and Jenny is back on her feet."

"That's what family is for," Uncle Pat responded and lifted her into a bear hug. "Besides, you're my favorite niece."

"I'm your only niece," Quinn laughed, "but I'll take it!"

Quinn was lucky and caught the bus back to her brownstone before it could pull away from the curb. She walked the few blocks home as the sun sank slowly beneath the horizon. She saw Zach sitting outside on the stoop and paused. He gazed up at the darkening sky. Quinn sat down on the step next to him. "Hey there, neighbor. Whatcha looking at?"

"Hey there, yourself. I'm watching Venus,"

Zach replied. He pointed at a bright spot in the sky. "See that bright star there? That's not actually a star. It's the planet Venus and right next to it is Jupiter."

"That's really cool. I always thought they were just stars in the sky."

"Most are, but you can see a few of the planets with the naked eye. I've got a telescope that Mrs. Garza said was okay if I set up on the roof sometimes, but its buried under a few more boxes."

"What got you into stargazing?" Quinn asked. She could smell the faint pleasant smell of his cologne. Something earthy with a touch of musk. She liked it.

"My parents took my sisters and I camping in Maine every year. My dad was an amateur astronomer, and we all learned about the different planets and stars. Maybe one day I'll do the same thing with my kids," Zach said.

"I think that's nice," Quinn said softly. "I wish my parents had taken me camping, but they were traveling so much that when they had a break, they didn't want to go anywhere."

"You've never gone camping?"

"Never. It's okay though, I had a pretty

decent childhood. I lived with my Grandma Rose while my parents were out on the road chasing down news stories. They're reporters. Grandma would tell me stories about growing up in Ireland and meeting my grandfather when he traveled to Dublin to study abroad a semester. They fell in love, and at the end of the semester, they married and moved here. I learned to cook and bake and I can drink a pint of Guinness with the best of ya," Quinn joked in an Irish brogue.

"I'll take you up on that challenge one day," Zach laughed. He reached over and brushed his hand across her cheek. "Sorry. You've got a bit of what looks like flour on your face."

Quinn wiped at her face and grinned. "It is. I got a job working at my uncle's restaurant, Hanrahan's, for the next few weeks. I'm filling in while the pastry chef recovers from a broken leg."

"That's good news. Uh, for you, not the chef, I mean. I've been to Hanrahan's before. It has the most amazing food. Your uncle owns it?"

"Yup. Patrick Hanrahan is my mom's brother. He and I spent time traveling all over Europe gathering recipes and cooking techniques so he could incorporate them into his restaurant."

"Forget camping. I'd love to eat my way through Europe. My cooking skills leave a lot to be desired. Thank goodness for take-out and TV dinners."

"Cooking's not hard. I could teach you a few basic things so you won't starve to death," Quinn offered.

"I'd like that. Maybe when I finally buy some pots and pans for my kitchen, you could start teaching me."

"Sure. What do you do? I never got a chance to ask the other day."

Zach started to answer, but the insistent buzz of Quinn's cell phone interrupted. Glancing down, she saw Indie's name on the screen. "I'm sorry, but I'd better answer. Indie's set me up on a date with some realtor for this weekend. She's calling me with the details."

"You'd better answer. It might be the date that changes your luck with love. I'll talk to you later," Zach said and stood up to walk back inside.

Quinn wiggled her fingers goodbye and punched answer on her phone. "Indie, before you tell me about the guy, let me tell you about my first day on the job." She glanced up at Zach as he entered their building. Had she imagined the disappointed look on his face when she mentioned her date? Shaking her head at the random thought, she started to tell Indie about baking bread, chocolate and Guinness.

CHAPTER SIX

Saturday afternoon, Quinn rushed home from Hanrahan's to get ready for her date that evening. Although she had sworn off dating, she found herself excited at the possibility that she might actually meet a nice guy. Indie refused to let Quinn know anything more about Paul.

"If I tell you anything, you'll come with a preconceived notion of what he's like. I want you to promise me you'll keep an open mind. From all of my background checks, he seems like a nice guy. No criminal history. No crazy exes posting threats on his Facebook. We're supposed to meet him at a club called Dark Dreams at eight. He said the club caters to an edgy clientele, so those leather pants Sean gave you are perfect," Indie informed Quinn that morning.

Now, Quinn held the leather pants in front of her and considered picking something else from her closet. Weren't leather pants retro? Maybe some black capris and a black lace blouse instead.

"No," Quinn said to herself. "You promised to try new things and change it up. So here goes nothing." She stepped into the pants and pulled them up and stopped. They were stuck on her thighs. She tugged them off and looked at the tag. They were a size ten which was her size. She'd actually dropped five pounds from the heat of working in the kitchen at the restaurant. Leather pants didn't have as much give as denim. Maybe she just needed to tug them up harder. She stepped into the pants again. This time she yanked hard when they got to her thighs. Although they came up to her hips, they were still a little too tight.

"Maybe I just need to put some lotion on my legs," Quinn said to her cat, Fat Panther. She walked into her bathroom and grabbed a tube off the counter. She tried to squeeze some into her hand. Only a small blob oozed out. Tossing it into the trash, she dug through her bathroom vanity looking for another tube. "Dang it! Any other time and I'd have fifty half-empty bottles of lotion, but when I need it…"

Quinn hurried into the kitchen. Maybe she had some by the sink for when she finished washing dishes. Aha! A small bottle sat next to the spigot. She pumped the spout a few times and a dried plug of lotion shot out followed by air. Twisting the lid off, she tapped it against her palm to eke out the last few dregs. Nothing but a small smear came out of the bottle. "Desperate times call for desperate measures." Quinn opened her refrigerator and pulled out a stick of butter. "A cook's best friend is butter and bacon grease. Let's see if they're right."

Quinn dashed back into her bedroom and unwrapped the stick of butter. She slowly swiped it from her ankles to her hips. Once she had completely covered her outer thighs, she tried the leather pants again. This time they slipped easily over her thighs. She grabbed a bottle of her favorite perfume from her bureau and spritzed it behind her ears and on her wrists. She sprayed some into the air in front of her and walked through the mist. "Just in case the butter smell comes through," Quinn said to the cat. Fat Panther gazed unblinking from his perch at the end of her bed. "Fatty, you don't understand the pressure of looking good when you're a girl. All you have to do is lick your butt and wash your paws and you are Joe Stud with the felines."

Quinn slipped on a ruby red silk blouse Sean had picked for her and buttoned it shut. A final critical look at her makeup and hair and she was ready to go. She was supposed to meet Indie out front at seven thirty, so she still had a few minutes to spare. She headed down the stairs at a leisurely pace determined not to mow Zach over again. As she came to the ground floor, she saw Mrs. Garza carrying two grocery bags and struggling to unlock her door. "Let me help," Quinn said, grabbing the bags of food.

"Gracias, *mija*. God did not mean for us to have more than two hands, but sometimes I wish he did. You look nice. Are you going on a date with a young man?"

"Thank you. Indie is taking me to a meet a guy. It's kind of a blind date."

Reyna Garza clucked her disapproval. "In Mexico, a young girl was courted by a man her family knew and approved of. Blind dates. Girls in my day did not go on blind dates, or if they did, it was kept secret. Young Americans want fireworks and romance. A relationship should not be about stars in a girl's eyes. I might be old, but I know a thing or two about love. *Más sabe el diablo por viejo que por diablo.* A relationship should be based on trust and friendship."

"You're right, Mrs. Garza, but I promised Indie I would at least meet this man," Quinn said.

"I have a handsome and single grandson you could date. He's a good boy and you're already friends."

"Um…but Sean's not really my type and I don't think I'm his," Quinn protested weakly. She wasn't going to be the one to tell her that her beloved grandson was a burlesque dancer who preferred the company of men rather than women. "Don't get me wrong. Sean's a great guy. He's funny, smart and handsome."

"Sean. If his mother knew he'd changed his name to sound more like a gringo, she'd be crying with the angels. Juan Carlos is a good name. It's a strong name for a strong man," Mrs. Garza huffed.

"Yes ma'am, it is," Quinn said as she eased towards the door. "I'm sorry, Mrs. Garza, but I'm going to be late meeting Indie. I'll see you later. Have a good evening."

Mrs. Garza made the sign of the cross over Quinn. "Be safe, *mija,* and don't cross Juan Carlos off your list yet."

Quinn hurried out the door before she said the wrong thing. Her timing was perfect. Indie pulled to the curb in her 1970 VW. Indie inherited Herbie the Love Bug from her parents. The commune had a van, so the car sat unused in a barn for years. Despite his many dents and scratches, he started every time and was great for parking in the crowded downtown parking lots.

"You look great!" Indie exclaimed. "Between the new hair and the clothes, your own mother might not recognize you."

"One can only hope," Quinn remarked. "I've ducked her calls for weeks now. She is livid over the Tad restaurant incident."

"She'll get over it. Twenty years from now."

"If she doesn't, she doesn't."

"Listen to you being independent and rebellious. You go, girl. We're supposed to meet Paul inside the club. Remember, he thinks you've been chatting with him online the whole time. I kept the conversations pretty neutral. He's allergic to shellfish, likes 1980s rock music and has a Bassett hound named Theodore."

"Sucks about the shellfish because I love

lobster and crab. I can live with the musical taste. Basset hounds smell bad. They're cute, but they smell like dog."

"Hello? They are dogs. Dogs smell like dogs. Cats smell like cats. I think they cover these facts in elementary school. Since I never went to elementary school, I could be wrong but…"

"You know what I mean. Some dogs smell worse than others. If I end up marrying the guy, my apartment will smell like Basset hound and be covered with slobber."

"Let's get through the first date before you start worrying about pets and living arrangements, shall we?" Indie turned onto a side street. She whipped Herbie into a parking spot that in Quinn's mind should only fit a bicycle. "The club's right down the street."

Quinn climbed out of the small car and checked her lip gloss in the side mirror. "I'll keep my mouth shut about the dog, but if he asks to bring Theodore over to my place, I can't be held liable for what Fat Panther does to it."

Indie laughed. "That cat could probably take down a grizzly bear." She walked down the street towards Dark Dreams. Quinn had to practically run to keep up. As short as Indie was, her little legs moved at a breakneck speed.

"Slow down! I'm going to be sweaty and out of breath by the time we get there," Quinn protested. "High heels are not my friend, but these pants would look silly with tennis shoes."

Indie waited for Quinn at the end of the block. "Quinn, what's up with that?" Indie pointed at the sidewalk behind Quinn. Quinn stopped and turned. When she did, two stray cats, who had clearly been following her, dashed up and began to lick her ankles.

"What the…? Get away!" Quinn nudged the cats away from her legs. "Ugh. I like cats, but this is ridiculous!"

"What are you? The cat whisperer?" Indie asked. "They won't stop trying to lick you."

"Oh crap on a cracker. You know what? It's the butter," Quinn said. She gently pushed the cats away again with her foot.

"Butter?"

"I couldn't get these pants over my thighs, and I was out of lotion. I used butter," Quinn explained. She tried to shoo the cats away with her hands. In desperation, she zigzagged down the sidewalk like a drunken sailor to confuse them.

Indie laughed and said, "I wish I had a video of that. It puts the butter on its skin. My grandma puts butter all over her Thanksgiving turkey. When we're done here, I can find a big oven and roast you like a Butterball."

"You're a laugh a minute. Thanks for reminding me of Silence of the Lambs right before I get ready to meet a potential date. Let's get inside before these cats make me their turkey dinner." Quinn yanked open the door of the club. As her eyes adjusted to the colored lights that pulsed in time with the music, Quinn glanced around her. "Oh, hell no. Toto, I don't think we're in Kansas anymore."

CHAPTER SEVEN

http://theromancereport.blogathon.com

A blog dedicated to the pursuit of love and happiness.

The Romance Report

Saturday, September 14, 1:05 a.m.

Here goes nothing. Since I recounted my European travel in my previous blog, Tales of a French-fried Foodie, I created this new blog, The Romance Report, to share my dating trials and tribulations.

Dating is not for the weak of heart. If I'd been a two-pack a day smoker in my fifties on her first blind date since her divorce, I'd be on the next boat to Alaska where the temperatures hover below thirty degrees the majority of the year. Clothes are your friend, dear readers! Please don't take them off in public and gyrate with others! I imagine the confused looks on your faces and promise to explain my love of parkas, long johns and lots and lots of layers.

Due to my dear, dear friend's (or frenemy after tonight!) machinations, I went on my first date courtesy of the dating site, True Hearts. My date, who I'll call Saul to protect his identity, passed the vetting process with flying colors. He's a successful realtor, loves animals and has no criminal background. A date, sight unseen, seemed perfectly harmless. Who knew that by the end of the night I would end up chained to a dungeon wall.

Thanks to a certain writer who shall remain unnamed, bondage has become quite the craze among the bored housewives and thirty-something singles here in the city of Richmond. Why, dear readers? I do not want to ever call a boyfriend, Sir. I certainly don't want him to spank me or vice versa. Ew!

Unbeknownst to me, my date's choice of club, Dark Dreams, caters to those who want a taste of the lifestyle without taking the full plunge. Imagine my surprise when my friend and I walked into the club and our eyes were assaulted by various and a sundry clubbers in leather chaps, bustiers which failed to boost, and creepy men in leather masks who will give me nightmares for the next fifty years. To my further dismay, my date, Saul, recognized me from my profile picture. He snagged me before I could turn tail and run. I assume he was as handsome in real life as he was in his photograph. I couldn't tell because of the leather eye mask he'd chosen as the accessory to his black leather vest and skin-tight jeans with a pair of handcuffs dangling from his belt. Gulp! I was waiting for him to go all Zorro and bring out the whip.

Saul tried to be charming. He really did. He bought me a Bloody Mary (a portent of things to come? Maybe.) He chatted with my friend and me about the real estate market, his dog, Peeadore, and his most recent vacation to Florida. Try as he might, I failed to succumb to his charms or laugh at his witty banter. Why? Behind him was a lovely couple who were slightly chunky. They liked to display their bodies like pork chops in a butcher shop. To top it off, Mr. Pork Chop kept snapping his small whip on his beloved Mrs. Chop's derriere which made her giggle and bray, "Oh, Marty, you bad, bad boy. I live to serve you."

Feeling slightly nauseous from the sweaty, half-naked bodies packed like sausages in leather casings, I excused myself to the ladies' room. As I fought my way past whips and chains, I made the mistake of catching some Marquis de Sade wannabe's eye. He grabbed my arm, slapped it in a wrist iron hanging from the wall and commanded me to beg. He wanted submission, but he got a swift kick in the groin and me screaming bloody murder instead. Fearing a lawsuit, management rescued me and offered free drinks to my date and me. I graciously declined their offer, grabbed my friend (frenemy) and slid my buttery butt all the way home (which is a story for another post.) Needless to say, dear readers, my quest for a life partner will no longer take place online. I'm off to the shower to wash the butter and the memories of Dark Dreams off of me. If I could only figure out a way to wash the vision of the Pork Chop couple from my memory. For now, sweet dreams and goodnight.

COMMENTS:

Britney11: I LOVE Dark Dreams. You should

give it another chance. It allows you to be you without fear.

QuinnieBee: I can be me without being naked and afraid in a club with whips and chains.

Dreambuilder: I want to know why you had butter all over you. Do tell.

QuinnieBee: One should always keep their house fully stocked with lotion when trying to wear tight leather pants. Enough said.

Dreambuilder: LOL. ☺

CHAPTER EIGHT

Quinn awoke the next day to her thirty-pound cat kneading the pillow next to her head and her cell phone ringing. Half awake, she fumbled and answered, "Hello? Whoever this is, it is way too early to call anyone on a Sunday morning."

"It's ten o'clock, Quinn, and it's about time you answered my call." The ice crystals practically formed on the phone as Quinn's mother spoke.

"Oops! Sorry, Mother. I was on a blind date last night and got in a little late." Quinn pushed Fat Panther off her bed and struggled to sit up. Stifling a yawn, she got up and scuffed her way into her kitchen to start coffee.

"A blind date? Interesting. You can't date the nice young man and family friend I set you up with, but you can trip the light fantastic with some stranger? What did this guy do for a living? Musician, street artist, mime?"

"No, Mother. He's a realtor. His name is

Paul, but I don't think I'll be going out with him again," Quinn set her cell phone down and poured herself a cup of coffee. Her mother's voice squawked through the phone. Quinn heard something about growing up and time to settle down. Blah, blah, blah. She added a spoonful of sugar and a dash of creamer, took a sip of her coffee, then picked up the phone. "Mom, I am a grown up. I have a job, my own apartment and don't want to settle down until I find the right guy. I don't plan on compromising just because he earns a good paycheck. There's more to life than money and career."

Her mother stayed silent so long that Quinn thought the call had dropped. "Mom? Are you still there?"

"I'm still here. Is that what you think I did? Married your dad for his money?"

Quinn sighed. No matter what she said, it was always wrong when it came to her mother. "No, Mom. I know you love Dad and that's why you married him. I'm just saying that a guy like Tad might earn a good living, but he's not a very nice person."

"I worry about you," her mom said softly. "I

want to know that you're married and settled down with a family and a career. I want you to be okay."

"I am okay. I've made a few poor choices in the guys I've dated in the past, but here's a happy thought. I didn't marry them! I like working with Uncle Patrick. It's giving me a chance to decide my next career move. And if the right guy comes along, I'll know. Tad wasn't the right guy."

"His dad's an ass, too."

"Mom!" Quinn exclaimed in shock. Her mother rarely cursed.

"Well, he is. It was actually T.K. that asked me to set you up with Tad. Turns out Tad has a habit of bringing strippers to company functions. T.K. hoped Tad would bring you to the next partner function. I didn't know any of this until afterwards."

"Are you serious? Oh my gosh! That's funny. Well, I don't feel bad about trying to hit him with my shoe then."

"Did you really throw your black Pradas at him? Those shoes aren't cheap, dear. You didn't damage them did you?"

"No. I actually hit the guy at the next table in the back of the head. That little move sealed the deal on getting fired."

Ann chuckled. "If it makes you feel any better, I got fired for from my first writing job, too. I called the editor of the paper an insufferable prig after he trashed one of my stories."

"Thanks, Mom."

"For what?" Her mother asked.

"For cheering me up," Quinn said.

"That's what moms do. Speaking of moms, the reason I called is about Grandma's birthday. Her seventieth birthday is next month, and your uncle and I wanted to have a big birthday bash at his restaurant. I need you to help me with the guest list and invitations."

"Sure. I'll come by the house later today and we'll come up with a list."

"Thanks, dear. You should wear the David Koma dress I gave you to the party. You can never go wrong with a little black dress."

Quinn rolled her eyes. "I'm sure you're right, Mother. I'll talk to you later." Quinn hung up and took a sip of her coffee. She grimaced. It had grown cold while she talked to her mom. She dumped it into the sink and poured another cup. Her uncle's restaurant was closed on Sundays, so Quinn planned to do laundry and go to the grocery store. Her cupboards had grown bare and she was down to canned soup and some moldy cheese.

Quinn showered and dressed in her favorite pair of jeans and a turquoise t-shirt on over her damp hair. Slipping her feet into an old pair of flip-flops, she opened her apartment door and found Zach standing in front of her.

"Oh! Hello. We almost had another run in," Quinn said with a smile.

"Good morning. Sorry to bother you, but I came to ask you a huge favor," Zach said.

"Sure. What do you need?"

"I have to go out of town for a week, and I wanted to see if you could feed my fish," Zach said. "If you could just stop by once a day and throw some fish flakes into the tank, it would be a huge help. Mrs. Garza offered to do it, but I know she has a hard time climbing the stairs, so…"

"No problem."

"Great. I appreciate it. Here's my spare key and the flakes are right next to the tank. I'll be back before the end of the week." Zach handed her the key to his apartment. "I've got to catch a flight this morning. Otherwise, I'd finally buy you that cup of coffee. When I get back?"

"Definitely. Have a safe flight," Quinn said. She closed and locked her apartment door behind her. "I'm off to restock my refrigerator. It's down to a block of cheese and a few stray crumbs."

"Thanks again. See you later," Zach said.

"See you later."

Quinn walked the five blocks to the closest market and grabbed a cart. She cruised up and down the aisles. She was looking at the selection of cat food when she heard a voice call her name. She glanced around and spotted a man pushing a cart towards her. He looked vaguely familiar, but she couldn't quite place the face.

"Quinn Daniels. How are you?" He gave her a wide smile showing his dazzling white teeth. "You don't remember me, do you?"

"I'm sorry. You look familiar but…"

"Doug Martin. We had Professor Djos' Intro to Journalism class together. Remember?"

"Yes! Oh my gosh. Doug, how are you?"

"I'm doing good. Ended up not going into journalism. Decided after Dr. Djos' brutal class that maybe journalism wasn't in the cards for me. Got my degree in teaching instead. Nowadays, I'm Mr.

Martin to a bunch of eighth-graders."

"Middle school? You're a brave man, Mr. Martin. Well, I stuck with journalism, but right now I'm helping my uncle out as a pastry chef at his restaurant."

"Married? Kids?" Doug asked.

"Nope. How about you?"

"Nah. I've been too busy with teaching. Listen, do you want to grab lunch? We could eat at the little café next door?"

"I've got all these groceries to get home, and I have to visit my parents this afternoon. Can I get a raincheck?"

"Sure. Let me get your phone number and maybe we could go out sometime."

"I'd like that," Quinn responded. She gave Doug a closer look. He was fit without being brawny, and his blue eyes sparkled in his lightly tanned face. She dug in her purse for a pen and piece of paper and jotted her phone number down for him.

He grinned and slipped it into his jeans. "I'll call you soon. It was good seeing you."

"Good seeing you, too. Talk to you later." Quinn turned back to her cart and a big smile spread across her face. A guy showed interest in her, and he wasn't a starving artist or a musician. She grabbed a bag of cat chow and tossed it in her cart. She decided to hit the hardware store when she was finished here. Maybe a little paint would add some flair to her apartment. Humming softly, she glided her way through the rest of her shopping.

CHAPTER NINE

Quinn spent Sunday afternoon painting her bedroom a bright shade of turquoise with cream paint on the crown molding. She decided to take a break at four o'clock and head over to her parent's house. She washed her paintbrush and roller and put them both in a plastic bag so she could finish the room the next evening. She walked the two blocks to where she parked her beat-up Volvo sedan. With limited parking in her neighborhood, Quinn usually rode the bus rather than drag Old Susannah out of her parking spot. Quinn patted her trusty metal steed on her dashboard when the engine turned over on the first try. Thirty minutes later, she pulled into her parent's circular driveway.

"Mom? Dad?" Quinn called out when she went inside.

"We're out on the deck, dear," her mother called from the rear of the house.

Quinn walked through the house and onto

the back deck to find her parents playing Scrabble and drinking iced tea.

"Who's winning?" Quinn asked, although she could guess the answer.

"Your father, of course, but I'm close enough to taste victory," Anne said. She laid down her tiles and cackled in delight. "Zephyrs. With triple word score that gives me a twenty point lead!"

"Lucky draw," Quinn's father drawled. He puffed on the cigar he had clenched between his teeth.

"Luck!" Anne squawked. "That, my dear husband, was skill and strategy. Oh my goodness. What in the world have you done to your hair?"

"I cut it and stripped the color back to my natural shade," Quinn replied. She waited for the barrage of criticism.

"I like it," her dad said. "It suits you."

"You look like Mama," Anne said softly.

"Does that mean you like it?"

"It means that you look like your Grandma Rose when you let your hair run wild like that," Anne said with a prim set of her lips.

Quinn sighed and sat down next to her mother. "I thought we were going to come up with a guest list for Grandma's birthday party. I can ask Uncle Patrick who he wants to add to the guest list when I go to work tomorrow."

"Your mother told me you're working for Patrick. Honey, I have connections and can get you a stringer job at the Times or one of the smaller local papers. Just say the word and it's done," David said with a snap of his fingers.

"I'm okay working for Uncle Pat, Dad. His pastry chef broke her leg so I'm helping him out for the next two months. After that, I'll figure it out."

"I'll go ahead and make a few phone calls and start laying the groundwork," her dad said. "Zigzag. That puts me back in the lead and leaving you in the dust."

"Drat!" Anne said, wrinkling her nose as she looked at her tiles. "Too many vowels on that last draw."

"Dad, don't make any calls yet. Give me time to figure out my next career move," Quinn begged.

"Fine, fine," her dad said with a distracted tone. "Where's the pitcher of tea? It's hotter than the blazes out here. I told you we should have put the shade umbrella up."

"It's in the kitchen. Why don't we all go

inside and get out of the heat. I call it quits on this game anyway," Anne said. She stood up and dumped her letters into the box.

"Another victory for David Daniels and the crowd goes wild," Quinn's dad made the sound of a crowd cheering.

"No one likes a sore winner, Dad," Quinn joked.

"Says the girl who has never won a game of Scrabble against her old man."

Quinn helped her mom pick up the game and carried the box into the kitchen. She pulled the pitcher of iced tea out of the refrigerator and after refilling her father's glass poured herself one. "So any idea how many people you want to invite to Grandma Rose's party?"

"The restaurant can't hold more than seventy-five people, so the party will be a little more intimate."

Quinn rolled her eyes mentally at her mother's definition of an intimate party. "We may want to see if any of Grandma's friends from bridge are able to come."

"Add their names to the list," Anne commanded as she put a pad of paper and a pen in front of Quinn. "I've already started contacting people. Once we get everyone's name down, we can pare it down if we need to."

Quinn perused the list of guests. "Mother, why do you have Tad on the guest list? Really? I doubt he'll want to come within five hundred miles of me after our dating fiasco a few weeks ago."

"Your father and his father have been hunting and fishing buddies for years. It would be rude not to invite them. I'm sure he'll decline, but the invitation has to be sent."

"Ugh. Well, if he shows up, I'm kidnapping Grandma and taking her club hopping for her birthday. I'm forewarning you now."

"I invited Marjorie Kellogg. Her son is in medical school and would be a catch."

"Casey Kellogg had the worst case of acne I'd ever seen in my life and he breathes through his mouth."

"Which is why he's going to be a dermatologist. He's a nice man. You could do worse."

"I doubt it. Anyway, I might bring a date of my own to the party. I ran into an old college friend today. He asked for my phone number and wants to take me out on a date."

"What does he do for a living? Something in the arts I'm assuming."

"No, Mother. He's not a musician or a starving artist. Doug's a middle school teacher. He's a nice guy."

"Hmm...well, I'm reserving judgment until I meet him."

"Your mother means until she interrogates him."

Quinn's mother glared at her husband. Rather than respond, she began adding names to the guest list. Fifteen minutes later, Quinn and her mother had a list of sixty guests. "Ask my brother who we've missed and call me tomorrow."

"I will. I better get back home. I promised to stop by my new neighbor's apartment and feed his fish while he's out of town. Fat Panther is probably starving anyway." Quinn grabbed her bag and after hugging her parents goodbye, she and Old Susannah chugged her way back to her apartment in Richmond.

She let herself into Zach's apartment with the key he'd given her. She fumbled her hand against the wall and found the light switch. Flipping it on, she stood momentarily transfixed. Although Zach's apartment mirrored hers, it couldn't be more different. Rather than the stark white walls like her own apartment, Zach had painted his living room vivid shades of blue. His walls were covered with paintings and photographs depicting scenes from nature and old buildings from around the world. She slowly moved her way around the living room. Her eyes traveled across the artwork as she tried to take it all in. She found herself transfixed by the images of Gothic cathedrals and towering spires on castles and mansions. She looked around the rest of the living room and spotted a drawing table covered with large pads of paper. Next to the table was an empty easel. An artist. Her new neighbor was an artist. Darn it. She was all set to like him. He was funny and good looking, but she was over the artistic, flaky guys. She looked around for the fish tank and saw it near the small television tucked into one corner of the living room. She moved across the room and opening the jar of fish food, she sprinkled a handful of flakes into the tank. Little silver flashes darted to the surface and sucked in the reddish-brown food.

"Here, fishy, fishy, fishy," Quinn cooed to

the tank full of small fish. She wasn't really a fish person. Too much trouble to clean the tank every week. Fat Panther would probably eat the fish anyway.

She glanced at the stack of movies next to the television. Zach's taste in movies were similar to hers. Comedies with a sprinkling of drama and suspense. The shelf behind the fish tank contained a number of books. Quinn scanned the spines and found interspersed with books on medieval architecture, some mysteries by authors she liked, too. Her eyes lit up when she saw the latest novel from one of her favorite mystery writers. She had the same novel sitting next to her bed.

Taking a last look around the apartment, Quinn had a brief pang of regret. Zach and she shared so many of the same interests. Shaking her head, she closed his apartment door behind her.

CHAPTER TEN

Quinn woke up at five a.m. on Monday morning. She planned to arrive at work early this morning so she could try a new recipe. She had been experimenting with tiramisu and wanted to make it and a traditional peach pie.

She did her morning yoga. She finished her routine and took a quick shower. Once dressed in a pair of jeans and a navy blue V-necked t-shirt, she poured herself a cup of coffee and turned on her computer to check her email. As she scanned her inbox, she was surprised to see it was flooded with comments forwarded from her new blog, The Romance Report. Many of the comments posted were supportive although a few made snide remarks. Pleased, she closed her laptop, fed Fat Panther and headed to work.

By noon, Quinn had finished making her desserts and had the rolls prepped to go into the oven. Monday nights were often the restaurant's slowest, so Quinn made a smaller batch. Her uncle arrived shortly after twelve to start prepping for dinner. He was thrilled with her desserts and Quinn felt a small rush of pride.

"I love baking. It makes me think of Grandma. Speaking of which, Mom wants you to call her and give her your list of guests for the big birthday celebration," Quinn informed him.

"I only have a few folks I want to make sure are invited. If I know your mother, she probably has a list of two hundred people written down and has to figure out who to offend and who she needs to curry favor."

"Not saying a word. I'm Switzerland when it comes to you and mom." Quinn held up her hands in mock self-defense. "I said I would ask and my duty here is done."

"It's fine. I have forty-five years of big sister self-defense under my belt," her uncle laughed.

"I bow to the master," Quinn made a gesture of obeisance.

"Quinn, I wanted to talk to you about an idea I've been kicking around in my head."

"Okay. What's up?"

"You have talent. Real talent and I'm not

talking about your writing. Don't get me wrong. I think you're a talented writer, but I think you should go to culinary school," Uncle Pat said.

"Oh, wow! I've never even thought about culinary school. I mean, Mom and Dad pretty much expect me to follow in their footsteps."

"I'm not saying being a journalist isn't a good career for you. What I'm saying is that you have a real gift in the kitchen. You always have. You love food. You love to cook. Maybe you would like to follow in your Uncle Pat's footsteps and become a chef."

"You really think I'm a good cook?"

"Definitely. I want to show you something." He walked into his office and a moment later came out with a newspaper and handed it to her. "Read Jacob Malachy's column."

Quinn started to read. It was a review of her uncle's restaurant. "Sounds like Jacob Malachy is a fan of Hanrahan's."

"Keep reading."

Quinn continued reading the article. Hanrahan's not only boasts a vibrant menu of fresh dishes sure to please even the most discerning palate, it serves the most delicious desserts this writer has had the pleasure to taste in some time. The chocolate orange cake melted in my mouth. It was a taste heaven here on earth.

"Quinnie Bee, Ma passed her gift in the kitchen to me and you. I'm not saying you need to make a decision or even go to school if that's not what you want. I want you to think about it. If you decide it's something you want to do, I'll pay for you to go."

"I can't let you do that, Uncle Pat," Quinn interrupted.

"I wasn't finished. I will pay for you to go to school with the condition that you come work for me afterwards for at least a year." Her uncle held up his hand to stop her from speaking. "Don't answer me right now. Take some time and think about it."

Quinn impulsively hugged her uncle and kissed him on the cheek. "You're the best uncle in the world."

"It's because I've been blessed to have the best niece." He patted her back and kissed her on her forehead. "Now go home and wash that flour out of your hair. You look like a bad imitation of a ghost."

"Will do!" Quinn brushed through her hair with her fingers. "See you later."

A half an hour later, Quinn arrived at the brownstone and found Indie waiting on the front steps. Her bright blue spikes bobbed in time to whatever music she was listening to on her IPod. Her eyes lit up when she spotted Quinn. She popped the earbuds out and hopped up off the step.

"What are you doing here?" Quinn asked.

"I stopped by the restaurant to give you a ride home and your uncle said I'd just missed you. Due to Herbie's turbo speed and light traffic, I made it here before you. You need to get cleaned up so we can head down to Espresso Yourself."

"Why?"

"We are going to experience speed dating," Indie said excitedly. "I've always wanted to try it. Sean called to say he saw a flyer posted when he bought his coffee there this morning. Best thing is that you only have two minutes to decide if he's a winner or a wiener. If he's not a catch, you have an easy escape."

"Ugh. Really? After the Dark Dreams fiasco, I don't know if I'm up to meeting a bunch of losers one right after another. I might go into overload."

"I promise you it will be a blast. Besides, the event only lasts an hour so we're there and done by eight. If you come with me, I'll treat you to Genova's Pizza beforehand," Indie wheedled.

"With mushrooms and olives on the pizza?"

"Of course. What kind of bribe would it be without?" Indie joked.

"Alright. I've got to feed the Zach's fish before we go out," Quinn said.

"Aren't we getting domestic and cozy with the hot new neighbor." Indie raised her eyebrows.

"It's not like that. First of all, he asked me to do him a favor and feed his fish while he's out of town for a week on business. Second of all, he's an artist so I'm so not going down that path again. No more poor, starving artists who need drama to feed their artistic angst. No more rock musicians begging for cash to get their guitars out of the pawn shop. No more broke deadbeats for me. From now on, I want a safe, responsible guy with a 401k."

"Sounds boring to me," Indie said dryly. "Not all artists are broke and not all musicians are jerks. You had a run of bad luck with two guys. To quote your Grandma Rose, don't throw the baby out with the bath water."

"Boring is what I'm looking for right now. Not everything has to be rainbows and unicorns," Quinn defended herself.

"If you say so," Indie followed Quinn up the stairs. "Personally, I love rainbows and unicorns. I think you should wear that orange top Sean picked out for you. It looks good on you."

"Orange isn't usually my go to choice, but maybe it will become my lucky color if I meet a nice guy tonight."

CHAPTER ELEVEN

http://theromancereport.blogathon.com

The Romance Report

A blog dedicated to the pursuit of love and happiness.

Monday, September 16, 9:17 p.m.

Dear readers, I knew I was right to be afraid when my dear frenemy returned with a proposal. "Let's try speed dating," she said. "It will be fun," she said. Well, let me enlighten you. Having a tooth pulled without Novocain is more fun. Stubbing your toe on a chair as you make your way to the bathroom in the dark of night is more fun. Listening to your friend's child play *Twinkle Twinkle Little Star* at their first violin recital is infinitely more fun. Well, you get the point.

The evening didn't start off too badly. I did

get a free pizza out of the deal. Frenemy (as she will now be forever named) and I shared a bottle of cabernet and a medium veggie pizza at my favorite pizza joint, Genova's, before heading to Espresso Yourself.

Some brilliant barista decided that speed dating hadn't completely died out and wanted to revive it at my favorite coffee spot. (If you haven't had their Mocha Monkey Chino, you are missing a coffee dessert explosion in your mouth. Try it. You'll thank me later.)

Frenemy and I arrived at the coffee house a few minutes before the torture was scheduled to start. The place was packed. To be honest, I was secretly glad that I wasn't the only person who needed help to get a decent date. Some of the guys there were good looking although there were a few duds in the crowd. Of course the first guy I was paired up with was a mini Donald Trump with a bad comb over and socks with sandals. The only people who wear socks with sandals are mental patients and prisoners. He was an accountant so my mother would have loved him despite his fashion faux pas. She would look at it as a challenge and opportunity to do a makeover. Downside (not including the sock/sandal disaster), he had the personality of a slug. I felt like a spreadsheet with my assets and liabilities being entered. From his reaction to me, I could tell he felt I had a negative balance. I gave a silent prayer of thanks when the timer buzzed and we changed tables.

Guy Number Two was a construction worker who was divorced twice, thirty and had three kids. Need I state the obvious. I'm not looking for love in that wrong place.

Now for the highlight of the evening. The frosting on the cupcake. The marshmallows in the hot cocoa. Guy Number Three or should I call him Inmate 5486955. Why you ask? Let me set the scene for you, dear reader.

"Hi, my name is Quinn."

"I'm Luke. Nice to meet you . You're too hot for speed dating."

"Ah, thanks." I blush and bat my eyelashes coyly because this guy is hot. Black hair. Blue eyes. Tight white t-shirt that showed his magnificent physique. I knew it was too good to be true.

"I'm a pastry chef and a journalist. Kind of trying to decide between the two. What do you do?"

"I'm looking for a job. I just got done doing a dime."

"A what?"

"A ten year stretch."

"Ah. So you were in the military? Cool. My grandfather was in the military. What branch of service?"

"Nah. Not the military. I just got done serving ten years in the state penitentiary. Armed robbery. But don't worry because I'm completely reformed. I got my G.E.D. and my college degree in marketing while inside. I'm ready to start a new life with a good woman by my side."

"Armed robbery," I squeaked. I searched frantically for a policeman, security guard, a granny with a gun in her purse.

"Don't freak on me. I'm serious about turning over a new leaf. Just ask my parole officer. You're gonna meet him. He's at the next table."

I didn't wait for the timer. I grabbed my purse, grabbed Frenemy and hit the door. I'm glad I didn't give the guy my last name. Even so, I put a chair under my front door for good measure.

Until next time, dear reader, goodnight and good luck in love.

Comments:

CourtneylovesTom: Yikes! I almost went to this tonight. Glad I dodged that bullet! Better luck next time.

QuinnieBee: Thanks. I don't think I'll try speed dating again. Not really my thing.

Shawnalovesboys: Girlfriend, did you wear that orange shirt I gave you because you would have had better luck if you had. Orange is lucky for love.

QuinnieBee: Yes, I did, and no, it clearly is not. Orange is also the color of the jumpsuits at the county jail. Hmm…Coincidence? I think not.

Grayson14: Hi. My friends and I saw your picture and if that's really you in the picture you're hot. We want to know why you can't get a date.

QuinnieBee: I ask myself that very question every day.

Grayson14: If you're still single when I'm a senior, will you go to prom with me?

QuinnieBee: Sure.

Grayson14: Do I get to touch you?

QuinnieBee: Isn't it past your bedtime?

Dreambuilder: So you like dark hair and blue eyes?

QuinnieBee: Not necessarily. I don't have a type when it comes to looks. I like a guy who is funny and smart. No artists. No musicians. Other than that, I'm not particular.

Dreambuilder: Good to know.

CHAPTER TWELVE

Quinn spent the rest of the week in a haze of flour, cocoa powder and yeast. Hanrahan's was booked solid for the week with reservations, so Quinn spent her afternoons and evenings that week sorting through her Grandma Rose's recipe box to add new items to her dessert repertoire. On Thursday afternoon, she decided to take a detour on her way home and went to Mary's Garden Home to visit her grandmother.

The assisted living apartments they had moved her Grandma Rose to were very nice. Each resident had their own apartment with a kitchenette; however, it was still difficult for Quinn to see Grandma Rose in new surroundings. She missed the scarred wooden floors and outdated cabinets of her Grandma's house. It was where she spent much of her childhood while her parents were busy working. Quinn, Grandma Rose and her Uncle Patrick would cook and sing up a storm in the evenings. Quinn knew every dirty Irish limerick and pub song much to her grandmother's chagrin and her uncle's amusement. Uncle Pat's sense of humor sometimes drove his mother to rap him gently on his knuckles with her wooden spoon and admonish him to "stop teaching the child to sing those dirty ditties!" Quinn smiled at the memory.

She knocked on her grandmother's apartment door. She waited a moment and knocked again. When she still had no answer, she headed to the community house in the center of the assisted living complex. Seniors could play cards, dance, watch movies or just sit and visit. Quinn knew her grandmother loved her card games. Hopefully she wasn't fleecing her fellow residents of their pensions.

She spotted her grandmother sitting with an older gentleman in the solarium. They were listening to music and appeared deep in conversation. Her grandmother's face lit up at the sight of her. Quinn leaned down and kissed her on her cheek, then sat down at the table.

"Quinnie Bee! What brings you to visit my tired, old bones on this beautiful fall afternoon?" Grandma Rose asked. "I'm glad of the visit, mind you. Gives me a break from all these old timers."

"Hey now. I'm one of those old timers!" The older gentleman sitting with Grandma Rose protested.

"Harold, I'm not talking about you." Grandma Rose patted him on the hand, then to Quinn said sotto voce, "Actually, I am."

Quinn grinned and held out her hand to Harold. "I'm Quinn Daniels, Rose's granddaughter. Nice to meet you."

"Harold Vogelstein. Pleasure to meet you, too. Nice to finally see a pretty face around here." He winked at Quinn, then turned an innocent face towards Rose.

"Touché. So, Quinnie Bee, what brings you out today?"

"Nothing special. Just missing you. I've been helping Uncle Pat out at the restaurant. He has me working as the pastry chef while Jenny recovers from a broken leg. I've been using some of your recipes."

"Patrick told me you'd been helping out. He also told me what a great job you're doing. I'm proud of you."

"Thanks, Grandma. I learned everything

from you." Quinn blushed at her grandmother's praise.

"He also told me he suggested you go to culinary school. Mind you, I never had to go to school to learn how to cook, but these days, a restaurant likes to hire someone with initials behind their name."

"I don't know. Mom and Dad spent so much money sending me to college. I think it would break their hearts if I chucked it all and became a chef."

"What do you want to do?" Grandma Rose asked.

Harold stood up and said, "I think I'll go get myself something to drink and let you ladies talk. It was a pleasure meeting you, Miss Daniels. Anytime you want to flirt with an old man, you come see me. It boosts my fragile ego after spending the afternoon with your grandmother." He gave Grandma Rose a cheeky grin and walked away.

"That man is incorrigible," Grandma Rose said, but Quinn could tell she was secretly pleased at the attention.

"So, what's up with this Harold character? Do I sense a little love connection?" Quinn asked, glad to delay talking about her future for even a few minutes.

"At my age? Certainly not!" Grandma Rose protested. "He's just a friend. We play cards together and talk about when we were young. Besides, he's too old for me."

"How old is he? Eighty?"

"He's sixty-seven, but if I'm going to have a late in life romance, I want them to be too young for Medicare. A girl has to have standards, you know."

"Grandma!" Quinn pretended to be shocked. Her grandfather had died in his early fifties from a heart attack. Her grandmother had been alone for a long time and Quinn had never heard her talk about another man. It actually pleased her to see a twinkle in her grandmother's eye when she joked with Harold.

"Enough about me. I'm old news, figuratively and literally. What's going on with you? How's your love life?"

"What love life? I finally broke up with the musician. I've decided no more artistic types. They might be fun and romantic, but it's like dating a teenager. No sense of responsibility."

"Responsibility is important, but you can be

responsible and still be romantic. Your grandfather used to save his pennies every week so once a month he could take me to the movies and buy me a single red rose. He made sure he paid the bills, but he also made sure he showed me how much he valued me."

"You never told me that," Quinn said. She didn't really know her grandfather since he had died when Quinn was just a little girl. Her grandmother would regale her with stories about his years working on the railroad and how poor they were when they were young, but she had never shared the softer side of her husband.

"Well, I think sometimes we fail to appreciate the little things the people we care about do for us. The important thing is to not take those things for granted because if you do, one day you'll miss them." Grandma Rose's pale blue eyes softened and she seemed far away for a minute.

"I don't think I've ever had anyone do little things for me like Grandpa did for you," Quinn said sadly. In fact, thinking back through her short list of relationships, Quinn seemed to do the pursuing and most of the work to keep the relationships going.

"Then you haven't found the right man, dear," Grandma Rose said. "You'll know he's a good man when he remembers the little things like how you drink your coffee and that you don't like Brussel sprouts or gravy. When they remember those little things, it tells you that they are invested in you and your happiness. Just make sure you're worthy of that investment. Don't ever take advantage of it."

"I won't," Quinn promised. She sat silently for a minute and gazed out the windows at the rose garden. "Grandma, do you think I should go to culinary school?"

"I think you need to do what makes you happy and stop worrying about what makes me, your uncle or your parents happy. At the end of the day, you have to look at yourself in the mirror. If you aren't doing right by yourself, then how can you do right by others?"

"I guess so. I need to think about it some more before I decide. It's a big step."

"I'm proud of you no matter what you decide to do," Grandma Rose leaned over and gave her a hug. "Now, on to more important matters. Have you made my strawberry rhubarb pie for

Hanrahan's yet?"

Quinn spent the rest of the afternoon into the early evening talking to her grandmother about different recipes. Her grandmother would offer her suggestions and Quinn faithfully jotted her hints into a small notebook she carried in her purse.

Later that evening as she sat reading on her couch, she thought about how much she enjoyed her day. She had spent the morning working in the restaurant creating desserts meant to top off people's evening out and hopefully, create memories. She had then spent the rest of her day reliving memories with her grandmother and creating new ones. She scratched Fat Panther behind his ears and whispered to him, "I hope that one day, I'll love someone as much as Grandma Rose loved Grandpa."

CHAPTER THIRTEEN

The next two days passed in a blur. Quinn took her grandmother's advice and made her strawberry rhubarb pie much to the delight of her uncle and the guests at his restaurant. On Saturday evening, Quinn came home and peeled off her dough-splattered jeans and put on a pair of faded black yoga pants and oversized t-shirt. She turned on her television and sat munching on a bag of potato chips. She was too tired to cook dinner. If she could motivate herself, she would get up a minute and fix herself a peanut butter and jelly sandwich.

A knock on her door, roused her from her couch potato state. Zach stood on her doorway with a brown paper bag in his hand.

"Hi! I see you made it back from your trip? How was it?" Quinn asked. She liked how he sported a little bit of a five o'clock shadow on his chin. It made him appear a little bit mysterious without being sketchy.

"It was busy but productive. I wanted to thank you for feeding my fish while I was gone, so I brought Chinese food. You haven't eaten yet, have you?" Zach held up the brown paper bag. Quinn could smell the food and her stomach growled loudly in response. "I guess not."

Quinn blushed in embarrassment. "I'm starving. I was so tired from work today that I was just going to make a peanut butter and jelly sandwich. You're a welcome sight."

"Stick and slide is great for lunch but doesn't cut it for dinner." Zach walked in and set the bag on the table. He pulled several white containers and some cellophane-wrapped egg rolls from the bag. "Where are your plates?"

"I'll get them." Quinn opened her cupboards and pulled out two plates. She grabbed some silverware and a pitcher of iced tea from her refrigerator. "Stick and slide?"

"That's what my mom used to call peanut butter and jelly sandwiches when we were kids," Zach explained. "The peanut butter is sticky, but the jelly is all ooey, gooey and slides across the bread."

"Ah. Makes sense. I don't think my mother

called them anything. Of course, my grandmother was the one who would pack my lunch for school and she would send enough to food for the entire class." Quinn opened the containers. She saw that he'd ordered one of her favorite dishes, Black Pepper Chicken. She scooped onto her plate and then handed the container to Zach. "You brought my favorite Chinese dish."

"Good. I took a stab in the dark. Since the drink you fixed me the other evening was spicy, I figured a spicy dish would be okay."

"You picked well," Quinn said and took a bite. "Mm mm…you have no idea how yummy this is right now. You are my hero."

"It was the least I could do. I really do appreciate you feeding the fish. They aren't much of a pet, but I like to look at them. I find them peaceful."

"Not a problem. Anytime you need a fish sitter, I'm your gal. Easiest job in the world."

"So how is the new job going?"

"Great! I love it! My desserts even got mentioned in a review of the restaurant."

"That's awesome. I'm still holding you to your promise to teach me to cook. Once I get done with this latest job, I'll be home more and you can teach me how to boil water."

"The key to great boiled water is in the water," Quinn said with a wise nod of her head. "I wasn't being nosy, but I saw you had the latest Christoff novel on your shelf. He is my all-time favorite writer."

"Mine, too. I always think I know who the criminal is, but I'll miss some vital clue and when I get to the end, it's always a surprise. You can never go wrong with a good suspense novel."

"Mystery and suspense are my favorite, too. Same thing with movies," Quinn said. She took another bite of her chicken. Her stomach rumbled in appreciation.

"I like a good suspense, but action comes in a close second. Don't tell anyone," Zach lowered his voice, "but I'm a huge Jackie Chan fan. Favorite actor of all-time."

"Really?" Quinn wrinkled her nose in puzzlement. "I like him okay, but I've only seen one or two of his films."

"He is underappreciated as an actor," Zach said seriously. "He does all his own stunts, he sings, produces, acts…he is a Chinese Renaissance man."

"If you say so," Quinn said with doubt.

"I tell you what, why don't I bring over one of his movies tomorrow evening and you can watch it with me. If you don't love him by the end, I will concede defeat."

"It's a deal," Quinn laughed. "I'll even make dinner."

"Score! Dinner by a famous chef and I get to watch my favorite movie." Zach raised a fist in triumph.

They spent the next hour eating and chatting about different books they had read and movies they both enjoyed. Quinn had to stifle a yawn near the end of dinner. Although Zach was good company, she was exhausted from the long week. "I'm sorry," she apologized. "It's not you. The restaurant has been booked all week, so I've been running around like crazy trying to bake enough rolls and desserts."

"I understand," Zach said. "I need to get going, anyway. I promised my buddy, Jeff, I'd meet him for drinks at the Dirty Dawg. He has some girl he wants me to meet. He's as bad as my sisters trying to set me up. Actually, it's his wife, Cindy, not Jeff. She seems to think that I can't take care of myself and I need a woman in my life."

"Well, you clearly need someone to cook for you," Quinn joked. She felt a slight twinge of jealousy at the thought of Zach sitting in a bar drinking cocktails with an attractive woman.

"I have the fastest speed dials for takeout in the city. Plus, I tip well, so I will never go hungry." Zach responded. "I'll see you tomorrow. Six o'clock good?"

"Perfect."

Zach stood up, washed his plate off and placed it in the drainer. Quinn followed him to the door and said her goodnights. Zach lingered for a moment in the doorway like he wanted to say something, but then with a nod at Quinn, he went down the stairs to his apartment.

Quinn plopped back down on her couch. She was full from dinner and content from the good conversation with Zach. He really was a nice guy. Thoughtful, too, unlike most of the guys she dated in the past. Not self-absorbed at all. Perhaps she would rethink her self-imposed moratorium on dating artists and musicians. But then she thought about how she had cried herself to sleep at night when her last boyfriend had repeatedly cancelled dates, borrowed money, then would come back with sweet words and promises that he would change. "Nope, Fat Panther. Nice guy or not, he is off the menu."

CHAPTER FOURTEEN

Sean Carlos and Indie showed up the next morning to drag Quinn out to brunch.

"I cannot believe you took her speed dating," Sean complained. "That is so early two thousand. The hot new thing is to exerdate."

"What in the world is exerdating?" Indie asked.

"You meet a guy and go on a date to a gym and workout together."

"Why in the world would I ever in a million years do that?" Quinn asked incredulously. "I mean, I am just so freaking attractive while I'm sweaty and trying to do lunges and squats. No guy wants that. Ever."

"You don't have to lift weights. You can go to a spin class, yoga, anything," Sean explained.

"I'm not downward facing dog with any guy on a first date," Indie said. "I'm saving that for marriage."

"That's funny!" Quinn snorted. "I might have gotten a date without any help from you two chuckleheads."

"Spill," Sean commanded.

"I ran into a guy I went to college with named Doug Martin. Nice guy. He's a middle school teacher now and is pretty cute. Anyway, he asked for my number, so I actually may have a date in the works with a decent guy."

"The realtor was a decent guy. He had weird proclivities in the bedroom, sure, but that was his only drawback," Indie protested.

"I'm sorry, but I'm not calling my boyfriend "Sir" and asking if I may please have another. Not happening," Quinn said emphatically.

"I am with you one hundred percent on this one, Quinn," Sean said.

"Are you ready to order?" Their waitress stood poised waiting for them to order.

"Coffee all around and for me, I'd like the sweet potato pancakes with maple syrup and butter," Quinn said. She closed her menu and handed it to the girl whose nametag said Angie.

"Sweet potato pancakes are just wrong on so many levels," Sean gagged. "What's wrong with good old American pancakes?"

"Says the Mexican crossdresser who pretends to be American," Indie laughed. "Leave Quinn alone. She has the palate of a food artist."

"Don't say artist," Quinn groaned. "A cute guy moves in and he has to be an artist. Why couldn't he be a banker or a doctor?"

"I like Zach," Sean said. "He's cute. He's polite to my *abuela* and he has good taste in clothes. If I was a single man, I'd be all over that like butter on pancakes."

"Give the waitress your order, Sean," Quinn said. "Sorry. My friends seem to think my love life is in need of fixing and can't focus on anything else."

"It's okay," Angie said. "I see and hear all sorts of weird things here. You should see the drama that happens on the graveyard shift. Nothing uglier than two people coming from a club after too much to drink and slobbering all over each other in a corner booth." She shivered in mock disgust.

"Great." Indie looked around with a leery gaze. She grabbed a napkin from the dispenser on the table and discreetly wiped the seat next to her.

"Don't worry," Angie said, "we wipe the booths down before we start the morning shift."

"Good to know," Quinn said.

"I'll take two eggs over easy, a rasher of bacon and rye toast. Oh, and a bowl of fruit," Indie ordered.

"Where do you put it all?" Sean asked. "I'll take oatmeal. I'm watching my girlish figure." He slid his hands down his slim sides.

"That all?" Angie asked. When they all said yes, she left to go turn in their order.

"Indie, you slay me. I can't even eat a peanut without gaining weight. It's a good thing I walk everywhere or I'd weigh five hundred pounds," Quinn said.

"So how's the pastry business?" Sean asked Quinn. He took a sip of the coffee Angie sat in front of him. He winced then grabbed the sugar container and proceeded to dump a half a cup of sugar into it. Satisfied, he took another sip, nodded and smiled. "Now that's a good cup of coffee."

"It's a miracle you don't go into sugar shock," Indie commented.

"Darling, I'm just a walking, talking box of sugary sweetness. Nothing's gonna hurt this delicious diva."

"Good grief," Quinn groaned. "I really like working at the restaurant. As a matter of fact, Uncle Patrick offered to pay for me to go to culinary school as long as I agreed to come back to work for him afterwards."

"You should do it," Sean said.

"Definitely," Indie agreed. "You're the best baker of breads and cakes I've ever met. It's a good thing I have a fast metabolism, otherwise I'd be the one weighing five hundred pounds from eating your pastries."

"Mom would be livid if I chucked journalism and went to work in a restaurant permanently."

"That alone should make you want to do it," Sean chuckled. "Girl, you've got to live your life to please yourself. You are twenty-six years old and look for your mama's approval like a ten-year old. It's not healthy."

"They spent a lot of money on my education. I don't want to disappoint them, either."

"Quinn, they are your parents. Even if you disappoint them, they are still going to love you," Indie said in a quiet voice. "You need to give your parents a little more credit."

"I know they'll still love me. I don't want to hear for the billionth time how my mother worked her way through college as a waitress and sacrificed so that she could give me a better life. Personally, I think life with Grandma Rose was pretty awesome."

"Well, I'm behind you one hundred percent if you decide to go back to school," Sean declared.

"Thanks. Change of subject. I think Quinn's Life under the Microscope needs a break, so I want to know what's going on with you two. Sean, any new guy on the horizon?"

"*Moi*? Like this diva's heart can belong to just one man."

Indie rolled her eyes. "Sean, you can't keep jumping from guy to guy. Don't you want to settle down? Date one guy? Have a little stability?"

"One day, sure, but I haven't met the one. The good guy shortage isn't just going on in the hetero world, you know."

"I found a nice guy," Indie said.

"What?" Quinn and Sean both exclaimed. Quinn leaned forward and fixed Indie with a penetrating gaze. "Spill it."

"He's a computer programmer and he works

at an insurance company downtown. He's a few years older. Never been married. No kids. Has a couple of cats, though."

"So basically a computer geek who lives alone with a bunch of cats. He's a male version of you!" Sean said.

"What's his name?" Quinn asked. "How long have you been dating? When you say older, how old? Geriatric age or hitting thirty?"

"Whoa. What's up with the third degree? It's like being around your mom."

"Burn!" Sean cackled.

"Hey, now that was just wrong. I'm curious about my friend's new love interest. I do not approve or disapprove."

"His name is Marty. He's thirty-two and we've only gone on two dates, but we have talked online every night for hours. He's funny and smart."

"So when do we get to meet him?" Sean asked.

"That might be a problem," Indie said.

"Why? Are you ashamed of us?"

"No, Sean, it's nothing like that. He's incredibly shy and when he gets nervous he stutters."

"We'll behave. Well, I will. I can't control She- Ra," Quinn jabbed a finger at Sean. "It's normal to get nervous around new people."

"It's not only new people. It's any people. He's much more comfortable behind a keyboard. The things he can type…"Indie said dreamily.

"TMI! Type dirty to me, darling," Sean joked.

The waitress arrived with their breakfast and the three of them were silent for a few minutes while they ate. Indie, as usual, finished first and with a sigh of satisfaction, she leaned back and patted her belly.

"I love bacon. Bacon for breakfast. Bacon for lunch. Bacon anytime. I do not know how in the world my parents have gone thirty years without eating meat. It's just wrong."

"You used to be a vegetarian." Quinn pointed out.

"Not by choice. They don't serve meat on the commune. I had to sneak meat from the other kids in high school. I couldn't swap lunches with anyone because nobody wanted my tofurkey sandwich on sprouted bread. Blech!"

"That doesn't even sound appetizing,"

Quinn said.

"Quinn, I forgot to tell you I made an appointment for you," Sean said between bites of his breakfast.

"An appointment? For what?"

"With the healer. If you want to change your luck, you need to remove the curse hovering over your love life."

"You know I don't believe in that kind of thing," Quinn protested.

Sean dabbed delicately at the corner of his mouth. "You may not be a believer now, but after you meet with my person, trust me when I say, you'll be convinced."

Quinn sighed, "I'll go, but only because it will make you happy and it will be the only way I'll have any peace from you."

"Like I would nag." Sean pursed his lips and fluttered his eyelashes at Quinn.

"Ha!" Indie scoffed. "I remember when you wanted me to go get a Brazilian wax. You nagged me every day until I caved in. Worst decision of my life, by the way. I'm still in therapy over the experience."

"Hmmm…I guess some people prefer to go

wild. Anyway, we are going to see Angelica next week. She's normally closed in the evenings, but since she's family she made an exception."

"Why not. Nothing else is working for me, so I may as well throw caution and common sense to the wind."

"That's the spirit!" Sean said.

Quinn shook her head. She doubted it would work, but in for a penny in for a pound.

CHAPTER FIFTEEN

After breakfast, Quinn headed back to her apartment to do laundry. Indie and Sean planned to spend the day shopping for a new wig for Shawna's new routine. Quinn grabbed a basket of colors and headed to the basement of the brownstone. She opened the door to the small laundry room and saw Zach was already there.

"Oops. I'll come back later," Quinn said.

"You don't need to do that. I tossed my load into the dryer, so by the time your load is done washing, it will be free."

"Cool. With just Sundays off, it's my only day to do laundry."

"You want to go grab the cup of coffee I promised while we wait?" Zach asked. He shut the door of the dryer, filled the coin slots with quarters and hit start.

Quinn hesitated. She liked Zach, but she didn't want to give him the wrong idea.

"Come on. I need some caffeine to help get me going this morning."

"Sure," Quinn relented. It was coffee, not commitment she told herself.

They walked to Espresso Yourself. The place was crowded, but Quinn managed to spot a vacant table in a far corner.

"You grab the table, and I'll get us some coffee," Zach said.

Quinn maneuvered her way through the café to the table and sat down. She heard her phone jingle in her purse. When she looked at the screen, she saw an unfamiliar number.

"Hello?"

"Hi, Quinn. It's me, Doug, from the other day in the grocery store. From Dr. Djos' class. Remember?"

"Oh, hi!" Quinn said. "I remember. How are you?"

"Good. Listen, the reason I'm calling is I got lucky and scored some last minute tickets to a show at the Altria and I wanted you to come with me. It's tonight. Do you want to go?"

"I'd love to go."

"Awesome. I'll pick you up at six, and we

can get some dinner beforehand. What's your address?"

Quinn gave him her address. "I'll see you tonight at six. Bye, Doug."

Zach set a cup of coffee down in front of her. "What's up?"

"Oh, a guy I went to college with called and wants to take me to the theater tonight."

"Guess we'll have to postpone our Jackie Chan movie fest," Zach said.

"Oh, crud! I completely forgot about watching a movie with you. I feel bad now," Quinn said.

"You'll have to bring me something you baked at work to make it up to me," Zach said. "No worries. We'll do it another time. I'm serious about the dessert from Hanrahan's though. I read a review in the paper the other day that said that whoever bakes the desserts is a genius."

"I'll definitely make you dessert. You read the review? I can't believe I even rated a mention. I've never even been to cooking school."

"Some people are born with a natural talent for things. I can draw but can't sing. My one sister has an amazing voice and could have pursued it professionally, but she decided to be an attorney instead. Susan said law feeds her body and music feeds her soul."

"I'm kind of at a crossroads myself on what to do. My uncle wants me to go to culinary school, but I'm not sure if I should. Both my parents are journalists. I've been working towards following in their footsteps since I was a teenager when I wrote my first story for the school paper. Cooking has always been a hobby, but I never considered it a career."

"Well, for what it's worth, I turned my hobby into a career. My parents wanted me to be a veterinarian or a pharmacist. Boring."

"Your parents are probably a little more understanding than my mother. Anne Daniels is not known for her open-minded acceptance."

"Really? That surprises me considering how much she's traveled covering stories around the world. I'm kind of a fan of your mom's," Zach admitted.

"Acceptance of others, yes. Acceptance of me wavering off the path she's laid out for me since birth, not so much."

"Parents always have high expectations of

their children. It doesn't mean they won't still support your decision to do your own thing. I followed my own path and I'm still my parent's favorite son," Zach said.

"Aren't you the only son? You told me you had two sisters but didn't mention brothers," Quinn pointed out.

"Well, there's that, but even so, I think my parents are proud of me for making my own way. They worry about me, of course, but once they realized I planned to make a go of my career, they decided to make peace with it."

"I haven't made a decision yet," Quinn said. "It's a huge step to completely rethink your career. Heck, my career in journalism started off with a fizzle. I think about all the money my parents spent on college and then I up and tell them, sorry mom and dad, I changed my mind. I'm going to cook for a living."

"I don't know what to tell you. You have to do what's right for you. No one else can live your life for you, but you can't live your life for anyone else either."

"That was mighty profound, neighbor." Quinn tipped her cup towards him in homage.

"Here's to life choices. Can't live with them. Can't live without them." Zach raised his coffee cup in a toast.

"Here here!" Quinn clinked her cup against his and laughed. "Thanks for being a sounding board."

"You're quite welcome. Any time you need to talk, you know where to find me. Bowled over in the stairway by my pretty upstairs neighbor."

Quinn blushed at the compliment. "We'd better get back and finish laundry. I've got to dig out something to wear to my date tonight."

Zach pushed back his chair and stood up. "Yeah. I'm supposed to go watch the game with my buddy. I have a feeling he's going to invite Dawn, the girl his wife Cindy had me meet the other night for drinks."

"I forgot to ask you how it went. Was she nice?" Quinn followed Zach out of the café and they wandered towards home.

"She's nice," Zach said hesitantly.

"But?"

"She was pretty. Actually, she was very pretty, but I don't know. She didn't have a lot of pizazz to her personality."

"Pizazz?"

"It was like swimming in the shallow end of the pool. No depth."

"Ah. I can see how that might be a problem. A hot girl whose nice, but not a lot going on upstairs. Every guy I know would love to date her."

"I'm not most guys. I would like to be able to discuss something more than the color of her toenail polish over coffee the next morning."

Zach held the door to the brownstone open for Quinn. "I think it's good you don't just look at the outside package. I'm starting to learn that lesson myself."

"A girl that doesn't just want a hot guy in a Speedo serving her margaritas on the beach? Be still my heart!" Zach joked.

"Hardy har har. For your information, no girl wants a guy in a Speedo. That's just wrong on so many levels." Quinn made her way down the stairs to the laundry. She looked over her shoulder. "I prefer my men in a pair of faded blue jeans and a white t-shirt. Simple and classic."

"Good to know."

CHAPTER SIXTEEN

"No. No. No. No." Quinn threw one outfit after another onto her bed. "I don't have anything to wear to the theater."

"You have a whole closet of new clothes that Sean gave you," Indie pointed out. "Surely something in that monstrous pile will do."

"Nothing that says elegant, sophisticated, funny and smart," Quinn complained. She slid hangers aside and dug into the back of her closet. "Aha! I'm wearing this." She held out the black dress she'd worn on her disastrous date with Tad. The drycleaner had performed a small miracle and removed the eau de shrimp scent that had lingered.

"I thought you were looking for a new you, not old Quinn."

"That doesn't mean I gave up everything black. The little black dress is essential to every girl's wardrobe. When in doubt, it goes from boardroom to Broadway with a spritz of cologne and a sassy scarf," Quinn said in a perfect imitation of her mother's voice.

"Okay, Stepford Girlfriend," Indie mocked and backed away with her hands held high. "I'm leaving on that note. Call me if you don't get home too late. If you don't make it home at all, call me with the juicy details tomorrow."

"That is not on my agenda for this evening. I'm looking for Mr. Right not Mr. Tonight Only, thank you very much."

"Gotcha. Well, I'm heading over to Marty's. We're going to write some code, watch a movie and stuff," Indie said as she opened the door to leave. "Do me a favor?"

"Yeah?"

"Relax and be yourself. I promise you that you'll have a much better time if you do." Indie slipped through the door and closed it behind her.

"Be myself. Ha! Like I know who I am at this point in my life, Fat Panther," Quinn said to the cat who had made his home on top of the pile of clothes on her bed. "I thought I was a journalist. Clearly not. I thought I had a hot guy who was romantic and sang beautiful songs to me while strumming his guitar. Partly right, but turns out he was a first-class toad, too. I don't know who I am or what I want right now You know what Fat Panther? I'm just throwing caution to the wind and going for broke. Whatever happens tonight happens. If it is meant to be, it will."

Fat Panther sat gazing at her with his large green eyes. He twitched his white-tipped tail at her. "You don't really care about this at all, do you?" Quinn sighed. "I'm wearing the dress and the heels. Maybe I'll have better luck with them this time."

Quinn showered and dried her hair, fluffing it with her fingertips until it fell in chestnut waves around her shoulders. She had splurged on some high-end makeup when she first landed her job at Under the Radar. She lined her eyes with an olive shade which made her gray eyes stand out. A light glaze of berry lip stain completed her look. Gazing at her reflection, she was pleased to notice her arms were more defined from lifting the large bags of flour at work. No turkey wing arms for her in the near future. Quinn slipped on the dreaded Prada heels, but this time slipped some foldable shoes into her bag.

She heard a light rap on her door, so she quickly checked her makeup and hair one last time and hurried to answer. Doug was outside with a single pink rose in his hand. Quinn invited him inside.

"I brought this for you," Doug said and handed her the rose. "Red seemed too bold. White said too Mommy. Pink seemed like a good choice. It says I think you're pretty and I want to date you, but I'm nervous and don't know what to say."

Quinn smiled and took the rose. She pulled a single stem vase out from one of her kitchen cabinets. "I think it's a good choice. Thank you."

"So, this is your place." Doug stuck his hands in his pockets and wandered around the living room. "I like it."

"I'm in the midst of redecorating. I haven't settled on a color yet."

"Black and white go with everything, but then you get the whole zebra thing. I like that you have the cool blue lamp and stuff. I still have the post-college bachelor pad theme going. If my roommate had his way, the whole place would be decorated in camouflage and beer posters."

"I guess my decorating isn't quite as bad as I thought then," Quinn joked. "I'm ready if you are."

"Do you like Japanese food?"

"I do."

"Great. I was a little nervous since it's not for everyone, but I remembered we all did sushi after one of our study breaks in college and you recommended different things for everyone to try."

"I can't believe you remembered," Quinn said.

"I have a confession to make," Doug said. He held the door open for Quinn. They made their way down the stairs to the front door. "I had a bit of a crush on you back then."

"Why didn't you ask me out?"

"You were dating some guy on the lacrosse team who will probably end up being a senator or somebody important. I'm just an average guy from a small town in southern Virginia."

"Well, he ended up being a first-class jerk, so he lost my vote if he does run. I kind of like average guys from small towns."

Doug flashed her a huge grin. With a flourish of his hand, he waved to the small sedan in front of him. "Your chariot awaits, madam."

Doug drove them to Yoshimoto's on Sandstone Avenue. Quinn was inwardly pleased when Doug took her suggestions on new dishes to try and he even recommended a white wine that he thought might go well with their choices.

Quinn laughed at Doug's stories of his middle school students' antics and she regaled him with stories of her travels with Uncle Patrick.

Later, as they drove to the Altria for the evening's performance, Doug maneuvered through the city's traffic while singing cheesy karaoke tunes from the nineties. Quinn laughed so hard she hiccupped.

"Stop! You're killing me," Quinn giggled. "Oh my gosh. Remember the time Tyler Owens ended up passed out and naked in the middle of the field?"

"Yes!" Doug said. "He didn't show his face for a week afterwards, poor guy. I'm glad it wasn't me. We had some crazy times, didn't we?"

"Yeah," Quinn said. She sobered slightly. "Sometimes I wish I could go back and be that carefree. I don't think I realized how hard it was going to be to figure out life and career and everything else after college. They should teach a class on that at the university. How to Survive After Graduation 101."

"Shoot," Doug said. "Half of our class would

have flunked out. I'm lucky. I realized I'd picked the wrong major and switched to education. Best decision I made."

"I thought I'd chosen the right career with journalism," Quinn said with a touch of regret.

"Hey now. No heavy thoughts on the first date. Rule number one of dating Doug. Date nights are for fun, not for deep thoughts," Doug commanded. He pulled into the theater's parking lot.

"So you're saying that you want shallow waters from your women," Quinn joked.

"I want my women to be puddles, not rivers," Doug shot back. "I like 'em purty without a lot of stuffin' in them thar heads."

"Oh, Dougie, you're so manly," Quinn said in her best imitation of Betty Boop.

"Thank you kindly, ma'am. I aim to please," Doug said in a cowboy drawl.

"Maybe we should both be on stage tonight with the rest of the actors because that was a first class performance."

"Thank you. Thank you very much."

"I'm having fun," Quinn said. They made their way quickly to their seats. The stage lights flashed to signal the show would begin soon.

"I am, too," Doug whispered. He reached over and grabbed her hand. Quinn glanced down, smiled and squeezed his hand.

The lights lowered in the theater and the curtain rose. It was show time.

CHAPTER SEVENTEEN

http://theromancereport.blogathon.com

The Romance Report

A blog dedicated to the pursuit of love and happiness.

Sunday, September 22, 11:55 p.m.

What a beautiful night dear readers! Who needs True Hearts? Not this girl! I had a great date with an old friend from college who I haven't seen in a few years.

D. and I ran into each other in the supermarket the other day. He asked for my number and a few days later, voila! We had dinner then went to the theater. It was comfortable. Like your favorite pair of jeans that fit just right even on your most bloated days.

So, dear readers, if you're looking for romance, don't go spend money on an online profile or dare to speed date with your local parolees. Pick a produce aisle and cruise. Lettuce all look for the one who makes us bananas next to the fresh tomatoes.

Signing off to enjoy some sweet dreams about D. McDreamy. Good night, dear readers, and good luck.

Comments:

IndigoRainbowUnicorn: I take it the date went well?

QuinnieBee: It was awesome sauce!

Dreambuilder: The problem with old jeans is that they are too comfortable. A little spark. A little pizazz. That's what I want in a girl.

QuinnieBee: Who asked you, anyway? Spark, shmark. I just want a nice guy who doesn't empty my bank account.

Dreambuilder: Comfortable jeans wear out and then what do you have? Holey pants.

QuinnieBee: Grrr…

CHAPTER EIGHTEEN

Quinn sprang out of bed the next morning. She should have been exhausted given the late night, but she felt strangely exhilarated. She, Quinn Daniels, went on a date with a guy who had a real job and was normal. Better yet, Doug asked her to go to a movie on her next day off. Quinn practically pirouetted into her kitchen to start her coffee. "Good morning, Fat Panther," she sang as she gave him an extra spoonful of his favorite canned food.

The day flew by at the restaurant. She made a simple peach pie with a side of homemade vanilla ice cream and a more elegant crème brulee for the second dessert choice. Her uncle had asked her opinion on the evening's menu choices and incorporated her idea for a simple roasted root vegetables as an accompaniment to his main dish.

"I'm still thinking about culinary school," Quinn told him.

"You have time. The next semester of classes

doesn't start for a few months, but you don't want to wait too long. If you decide to go, we'll need to get your application in and your spot reserved. Fortunately for you, I happen to know someone at the school." Uncle Pat winked at her.

"I want to go, but I still have bills to pay. I'm not moving back in with Mom and Dad."

"Let me worry about that. I have a few tricks up my sleeve yet."

"I don't want to take money from you. Tuition is a big enough gift. I can't ask you to do anything else."

"It's not a gift, QuinnieBee. You will be my indentured servant for at least a year afterwards which guarantees me a successful restaurant with you on my staff."

"Hmm…I don't know about all of that. I got lucky with a reviewer who liked my cake. It doesn't make me a chef."

"Don't sell yourself short. There's more to you than meets the eye. Hanrahan blood runs through your veins. Hanrahans are fighters and survivors. Look at Ma and all she went through with Da," Patrick said.

"All she went through?" Quinn was

confused. Her Grandma Rose had nothing but the highest praise for Quinn's grandfather. Although she didn't remember him, Quinn could picture him in her mind from all of the stories she'd been told growing up in her grandmother's kitchen.

"Ma lived through some hard scrabble years. We all did. Why do you think your mother's such a pain in the…well, so uptight? We lived off free cheese and baloney many a night while Da was out of work."

"I thought Grandpa worked on the railroads and made good money."

"He did when we were older, but when we were little, he worked as a bartender and musician. Ma used to take in ironing and clean other ladies' houses in order to make ends meet. Your mother wore hand me downs from some of her classmates. Clothes given to Ma when she cleaned houses. Your grandmother never complained, but I remember her sitting up at night sewing in her favorite chair. She would try to alter the clothes for your mother so the other girls wouldn't know they were hand me downs."

"I never knew," Quinn said softly. Her grandmother had never said one unkind word about her husband.

"Well, now you do. We Hanrahans come from the best Irish stock. We're strong and smart. We don't always start out okay, but in the end, we always survive. A little battle scarred and tired but that's part of life."

Quinn thought about what her uncle had told her as she boarded the bus for home. She decided to hop off the bus and take a detour to visit Grandma Rose.

Quinn found her grandmother in her small apartment. She was fixing herself a pot of tea and grabbed another cup for Quinn.

"Two visits in less than two weeks! I must be ill or something," Grandma Rose joked.

"I hope not," Quinn replied. "Uncle Patrick and I were talking about Grandpa today. How come you never told me how tough it was when you were first married?"

"It wasn't tough. We had some tight times, but we had each other. We knew that no matter what happened, the two of us would stand together and face whatever troubles came."

"Uncle Patrick said Grandpa used to play music and tend bar."

"He did. He played guitar and could sing the pants off an angel," Grandma Rose said.

"Grandma!" Quinn laughed.

"It's true," Grandma said. "He was talented, but not good enough to really do it professionally. I thought it would break his heart to quit playing, but he said as long as he had me and the children, he would always have a song in his heart."

"Why did he stop playing?" Quinn asked.

"One night he came home from the bar and found me crying. I didn't have enough money to pay the gas bill and buy food. I couldn't decide whether to make sure my children weren't cold or make sure they had food. Your grandpa went the next day and pawned his guitar and applied for a job on the railroad. Anne and Patrick had heat and food that month."

"Did he ever get his guitar back?"

"Aye, he did. He never knew, but I went and borrowed the money from one of the nice ladies I cleaned houses for. I promised to bake her dessert every week for a month in exchange. I went and got his guitar out of the pawn shop. He didn't ask where the money came from, and I didn't tell him."

"Maybe I shouldn't have sworn completely

off musicians and artists. Grandpa turned out okay."

"It's not what they do for a living, dear, that makes the difference. It's how they do their living that's important."

"Huh? I don't get it." Quinn's face screwed up in confusion.

"Your grandpa made home and family the priority. We could have stayed poor as church mice the rest of their lives, but we would have still be happy because we treated each other with respect. It's when the person you're with doesn't value who you are and what you stand for as a person that it falls apart. You could be a Rockefeller with all the money in the world, but if you're poor in spirit, then you aren't worth a plug nickel as far as I'm concerned."

Quinn sat quietly and thought about what her grandmother had said. "I guess you're right. It wasn't so much that Johnny was a guitarist that was the problem. My hard work and my time weren't important to him. My feelings and my time didn't have value to him. It's probably why he didn't think twice about taking my stuff. Thanks, Grandma."

"You're welcome. My old bones might not be as tough as they used to be, but I still know a few things."

Quinn stood up and kissed her grandmother on her cheek. "I think you know a lot of things, Grandma. I'd better get home. The jungle cat I live with will be squalling at the door for his dinner if I'm too late."

"Come see me again anytime, sweetheart."

Quinn left and headed towards home. Her head was spinning from the night before and the revelations from her family. She realized life and love weren't quite as easy as they appeared on the thirty minute sitcoms she'd watched growing up. If she lived to be one hundred, she might just figure out life and men.

CHAPTER NINETEEN

http://theromancereport.blogathon.com

The Romance Report

A blog dedicated to the pursuit of love and happiness.

Monday, September 23, 3:37 p.m.

Hello, dear readers. No, I haven't gone on another date. I just wanted to share what I learned from the wisest woman I know, my grandmother. A guy is a keeper if he remembers that you take two spoons of sugar and a little cream in your coffee. A guy is a keeper if he gives you the last bite of his favorite piece of pie. A guy is a keeper if he'll put your needs in front of his wants. Now notice what I said, dear readers, your needs in front of his wants. That means sacrifice. It's a hard thing for any person to do sometimes, but if he's the one, he will be willing to sacrifice. Now this doesn't mean he'll give up his existence to make you happy. It also doesn't mean you don't have to be willing to do the same for him. Grandma taught me that when you love someone, you make them a priority in your life. I've decided to listen to my beautiful Grandma because she is the wisest woman I know. I want to be a priority in someone's life, not an afterthought. Wish me luck, dear readers, as I look for the guy that thinks I'm number one.

Comments:

Sleepingbeautiful89: I know just what you're talking about, girl. I dated a guy that put his pet ferret before me.

QuinnieBee: Wow! A ferret. Really? At least it's alive. My last guy put a guitar on my side of the bed because he didn't want it to get scratched leaning in a corner. I slept on the couch.

Sleepingbeautiful89: Ouch!

CHAPTER TWENTY

Quinn was disappointed that she hadn't heard from Doug yet. She knew he taught school, but she had to admit that she secretly wished he'd taken a moment and texted her. She sighed and decided a quick bike ride at the park would get her blood flowing and her energy level back so she could start painting her bathroom. She'd chosen a pale dove gray for the walls with pale lavender towels and vanity set to offset the gray. She loved the color combination, but she dreaded taping all of the bathroom fixtures to keep from getting paint on them. It was her least favorite task. Now if she could get a guy to do that for her, she would have it made.

Quinn walked into the backyard to the small shed where she kept her bicycle. It was a turquoise Schwinn with a basket on the front and she had named it Maddie after her favorite doll as a child. Quinn was a firm believer in naming cars and bicycles. She thought it made the car more likely to start and the bicycle less likely to get a flat tire. She wheeled it to the back gate.

"Hey! Quinn! Where are you headed?" Quinn whipped her head around and saw Zach leaning out his apartment window waving to her. "Hold on a second. I'll be right down."

Quinn parked her bike and waited until Zach came running through the backyard to where she stood. "What's going on?" she asked.

"I need the biggest favor in the world. If you do this for me, I'll owe you for the next year. I'll wash your windows, fold your laundry, anything."

"Help me paint my bathroom?"

"If you do this for me, then yes," Zach said earnestly.

"Oh boy. This must be huge. I won't help you dispose of a body or anything illegal," Quinn warned, only half in jest.

"No. Nothing like that. I need you to go with me to a dinner party at my buddy's house on Wednesday," Zach said.

"A dinner party? Is that all? Shoot. You could have gotten me to do it with a cheap cup of coffee," Quinn said with relief. "I thought it was going to be something awful."

"Well, I haven't gotten to the favor part. I need you to pretend we're a little more than neighbors, a little less than girlfriend and boyfriend." Zach gave her a rueful look. "I begged off another date with Cindy's friend by telling them that you and I were kind of starting to see each other."

"You lied," Quinn said flatly.

"Well, yeah. But this girl was circling me like a shark around chum and I panicked. I told her I was interested in somebody else because I didn't want to hurt her feelings. She told Cindy, Cindy told Jeff and now I'm toast if I don't produce a living, breathing female. Please. I'll paint your kitchen, too."

Quinn narrowed her eyes. "I want kitchen, bathroom and living room painted or I will throw you under the bus, my friend."

"Deal. You drive a hard bargain," Zach held out his hand. Quinn took it and shook. She felt a slight shock when his hand closed around hers. Static electricity, she thought. I need to start using fabric softener on my laundry.

"So how many dates have we gone on?"

Quinn asked, crossing her arms and leaning against the fence.

"Only two official dates, but we talk all the time and hang out in each other's apartment every evening. We went for coffee and then I took you rock climbing," Zach said.

"Rock climbing? Are you out of your mind? Do I look like I've ever gone rock climbing?" Quinn sputtered. She uncrossed her arms and grabbed her bike. "I don't know if you should take me as your alleged "dating friend" or not. I'm not a very good liar."

"You won't be lying."

"Didn't you hear what I said. I've never climbed a rock in my life. A tree, yes. A cliff, not on your life." Quinn put her bike helmet on and fastened the clip under her chin.

"Well, it wouldn't be a lie if you went with me today," Zach replied. "If you wait ten minutes, I'll grab my bike and we can ride down to the park. They put in a climbing gym a few blocks away from there, so after we do a few laps through the park, we can go climb a wall."

Quinn shook her head. "I don't know. I've never done it before. I'm a little scared of heights."

"Weren't you the girl that just underwent Operation Quinnover or Quinn 3.8 or some such thing the other day? You can spread your wings a little more and come climbing with me. If you hate it, I'll buy you dinner," Zach offered.

"How about you buy me dinner whether I like it or not?" Quinn shot back. Quinn straightened her shoulders and met his gaze. "The new Quinn wants a little more pampering and a lot less pandering in her life."

"You really are a tough negotiator, but alright. Give me time to make a quick call to Jeff and Cindy and confirm that we'll be there and grab my bike. I'll be back."

Zach sprinted back inside the brownstone. Quinn couldn't help but notice his tanned legs and the way the afternoon sun glinted off his hair. She shook her head. "I want a nice, normal guy with a normal job. Plus, what kind of guy climbs rocks for fun?"

Less than ten minutes later, they were biking their way down a side street to the nearby park. Quinn raced ahead of Zach and when she thought she had a solid lead on him, she slowed her pedaling only to have him zip by on his ten-speed.

"Pedal, pedal, as fast you can. You can't catch me, I'm a ten-speed man!" Zach called over his shoulder.

"My Maddie might be slower, but I can haul a snack in my bike basket. Guess Mr. Ten-Speed Man didn't count on that!"

Zach skidded to a stop and waited for Quinn to catch up. Once she neared him, she circled his bike around her. "So, Miss Quinn, what kind of snacks did you bring with you to the park?"

"Chocolate chip cookies with cherries. I might have brought an extra one that I'd be willing to share with the right person."

"Hmm…and what makes this person worthy of said cookie?"

"Oh, I don't know," Quinn said with a coy smile. "Can you let me look through your telescope one night?"

"Not on a second date! What kind of guy do you think I am?" Zach pretended to be shocked. He gave her a sly look. "Maybe on a third date."

"I'm counting that dinner party as a third date."

"Fair enough," Zach said. "But I'm still not letting you beat me." He zipped ahead of her again.

Quinn laughed and pedaled faster.

They spent the next twenty minutes circling the park. On their final lap, Zach took a side path and led Quinn to the newly-constructed climbing gym. She took off her helmet and fluffed her flattened hair.

"I must have helmet hair," she said, running her fingers through her waves again.

"It's a look. You're pretty enough to carry it off," Zach said.

"Ah, thanks. Every girl wants to know she looks gorgeous with hat hair."

Zach paid their entrance fee and picked out their equipment. He spent several minutes going over safety and showing Quinn how to attach herself to the safety line. The staff person working the wall made sure they were both securely attached.

"You want to look up, not down. If you look down, you'll get scared and it might make you lose your grip," Zach explained.

"Keep my eye on the prize," Quinn nodded. "Got it."

"I'll go a little bit ahead of you, so you can see how it's done." Zach stepped to the wall and grasped the small handholds jutting from the wall. "I try to look and see what the best direction for my reach and height is. The best way to climb isn't always straight up. Sometimes you have to make a little side journey."

"Are we talking about climbing or life?" Quinn called after him. She watched him crabwalk his way to the side and held her breath as he leaped to the left and swung on his rope to reach a handhold.

"Both!" He called down to her. "Okay, now your turn to start."

"Here goes nothing," Quinn muttered to herself. She reached out and grabbed a small handhold and pulled herself up. Soon she found her rhythm and started to grasp and pull herself upwards. "I've got it!"

"Great job! Now the goal is to reach the top. Then I'll show you how to get down."

When Zach said the word "down" Quinn made the mistake of looking down at the ground. She froze. She hadn't realized how far up she was. The ground seemed to roll and sway underneath her, but she realized it was her head that was swaying back and forth as dizziness took hold.

"Zach! I looked down!" Quinn shouted, fright causing her voice to crack. She squeezed her eyes shut.

"Hold on! I'll come down to you."

"You guys okay?" The young guy manning the wall called up to them.

"She's fine. I'm going to help her out," Zach called to the staff. The guy responded with a thumbs up.

Quinn clung to her small handhold, but her fingers started to cramp. After what seemed hours, but was probably only a minute, Zach zipped down next to her. "I want you to look at me, Quinn. Open your eyes and look at me."

Quinn opened her eyes and her gray eyes met his bright blue ones. "I don't want to fall," she squeaked.

"Listen to me, Quinn. You're not going to fall. You and I are going to climb to the top of this wall together. I won't ever leave your side," Zach said with a reassuring smile. "Just do what I do, and you'll be fine. I promise."

"I'm scared."

"There's nothing to be scared of, Quinn. I'm right here. I'm going to start climbing and you're going to put your hands and feet where I put mine. Okay?"

"Okay." Quinn sniffled a little.

"Hey. The new Quinn is tough and can do anything she wants."

"New Quinn. Tough. Gotcha." Quinn screwed up her courage and as Zach climbed in front of her, she followed behind him. A few minutes later, he stopped. "What did you stop for?"

"We've reached the top," Zach grinned.

"Really? I made it all the way to the top?" Quinn gasped. She was too scared to look down, but when she looked up, she realized that she was out of wall. "Alright! Now how do I get down?"

Zach laughed. "Getting down is a whole lot easier than getting up. You'll rappel down. First you call down to the guy holding your safety line to let him know you're heading down. Belay!"

Quinn watched as Zach pushed himself away from the wall and quickly let out some of his rope as he rappelled his way down the wall. Soon she spotted him on the ground.

She closed her eyes, took a deep breath and pushed off. Miraculously, she didn't plummet to her death and after a few bad starts, learned how to push herself off the wall while slackening her rope. Eventually, her feet touched the ground.

"I did it! Oh my gosh! I really did it! I climbed all the way to the top and then I zipped myself all the way back down!" She jumped up and down excitedly, clapping her hands.

Zach hugged her and smiled. "Yes, you did. I'm proud of you. It's a little intimidating climbing for the first time. Your arms and legs are going to hurt tomorrow. It takes muscles you don't realize you have."

"I can't believe I went climbing. The old Quinn wouldn't have done it. I'm shaking!" Quinn laughed and held her hand out and showed Zach.

"It's your muscles. I tell you what. Instead of going to dinner, why don't we stop by Salvatore's Deli on the way home and pick up some food. We can eat dinner on the rooftop and I'll show you my telescope."

"Why, Zach, are you showing me your telescope on a second date? The neighbors might talk!"

"I'll risk it," Zach winked at her. "Come on, Mighty Quinn, let me feed you. You earned dinner and dessert."

"I most certainly did," Quinn agreed. She hopped on Maddie and led the way home.

CHAPTER TWENTY-ONE

Zach and Quinn picked up sandwiches at the deli and rode the few remaining blocks home. When Quinn started to climb the stairs to her apartment, she gave a sharp gasp of pain. Holy cow her calves hurt!

"After we eat, you should soak in a warm bath with Epsom salt," Zach advised her. "Here, I'll help you up the stairs. I promise it will only hurt for a few days."

"Great. How come you're not praying for an early death from pain?" Quinn grumbled.

"I go climbing at least once a week. With my job, I have to be able to climb around in tight spaces and so I do rock climb for fun and for work."

"Artists climb rocks? What are you? Some kind of New Age artist or something?" Quinn was confused. She tried to imagine Zach painting while climbing around on a large canvas.

"What made you think I was an artist? I do

historic restoration of buildings," Zach said.

"Oh." Quinn felt her face grow hot with embarrassment and confusion. "Um…I saw drawings in your apartment when I fed your fish. I assumed you worked as an artist."

Zach laughed. "I like food too much to starve for my art. No, I'm not an artist although I do draw and paint as a hobby. I actually own my own company, Taylor Historical Restorations. I work from home when I'm not on site."

Quinn opened the door to her apartment and Zach helped her hobble to her couch. She plopped down and sighed as her calves went from screaming to a constant whimper. "Ah. Sweet relief. Historical restoration sounds interesting, but how come you rock climb for work?"

"Have you ever been on the outside of a two-hundred year old church steeple? You need to have no fear of heights and you better know how to get down from the outside if you need to. A lot of my work comes from historical associations and churches. I'm an architect with a background in art history. I even work on cemetery mausoleums sometimes."

"I'm impressed. Here I thought you were a

starving artist, and you're an actual professional with a real career and everything," Quinn said. She struggled to get up. "Let me grab some plates and we can eat those sandwiches. I'm starving."

Zach motioned for her to stay put. "I'll get the plates and sandwiches. Just point me in the right direction. Kitchens and I may not be on a first name basis, but I can plate a sandwich. I travel a lot so the need to cook rarely comes into play."

Quinn told him where her plates were. A few minutes later, Zach presented her with a sandwich, chips and a large pickle spear. "One roast beef sandwich with horseradish. What would you like to drink?"

"There's a bottle of white wine chilling in my refrigerator. Do you mind opening it and pouring me a glass? Maybe it will relax my muscles."

"I live to serve beautiful women." Zach bowed and went back into the kitchen. A moment later he returned with two glasses of wine and his sandwich on a plate balanced on his forearm.

"Uncle Patrick needs you to work at the restaurant," Quinn observed. She took a big bite of her sandwich. It was delicious. It had just the right amount of horseradish and cheddar cheese to light up her taste buds without overwhelming the roast beef.

"I waited tables in college. I was lucky enough to get a scholarship to pay my tuition, but I needed spending money. I got a job at a local pizza place," Zach explained. "Good sandwich. I'm glad you suggested I try the Muenster cheese. I've never had it. I've always been a Swiss or American cheese kind of guy. Simple tastes."

"Stick with me and you won't go wrong."

"Deal. Quinn, you really impressed me out on the wall. You were scared and you could've gone back down, but you didn't."

"I'm actually impressed with myself. A few months ago, I wouldn't have even tried to climb that wall. Thanks for taking me."

"Here's to Quinn 2.0." Zach raised his glass of wine.

"To Quinn 2.0," Quinn agreed, touching her wine glass to his.

They say in companionable silence for the next few minutes eating their sandwiches. Quinn felt comfortable sitting on her couch next to him. She ate the last bite of her sandwich and picked up her pickle. "No sandwich is complete without a dill pickle wrapped in paper to top it all off."

"Agreed. I couldn't date a girl who gave me her pickle. It shows a complete lack of character and taste," Zach joked. "I'll give you a raincheck on the telescope. Why don't we save that until next weekend when you aren't hobbling around like a ninety-year old."

"Hey. I'm not in that bad of shape. Lifting big sacks of flour and sugar at the restaurant keep me in prime fighting condition." Quinn held her fists up and circled them around like a boxer. "I don't want to climb the ladder to the rooftop right now though. I doubt I could grasp the rungs."

"I warned you that climbing would find muscles you didn't know you had."

"I could have gone a lifetime without meeting those muscles."

"Does that mean you won't go climbing with me again?"

"Nope. It means next time, I'll be better prepared."

Zach's face broke into a grin. "If you're serious, I can take you climbing on some real cliffs down by the Chesapeake Bay. It's about a two hour drive from here, but it is well worth it."

"Whoa. Slow down. Let me work my way up to the real climbing. For right now, I'll stick with the plastic wall and the safety mat," Quinn said.

"I'd better get going and let you go soak your legs." He stood up and gathered up their plates to take to the kitchen. "I'll see you later, Quinn. Thanks for spending the afternoon with me. It was nice."

Later, as Quinn sat soaking in the hottest water she could stand with some lavender-infused Epsom salt, she thought about Zach. Not an artist, she mused.

CHAPTER TWENTY-TWO

Quinn crawled her way out of bed the next morning. Although the hot bath had helped, she still hurt in her legs and upper arms. She knew the day was going to be a tough one at work. Downing two ibuprofen, she grabbed a protein bar and poured some juice into a to-go cup. If she was going to climb a cliff wall with Zach she needed to get into better shape. She grabbed her purse and keys and realized that she didn't have her cell phone. Searching her apartment, she found it had dropped between her sofa cushions. The low battery warning blinked at her. She had two text messages. The first one was from Doug. She opened it.

"Hi. Had a great time on our date. I can't wait to see you again this weekend." Quinn did a little foot dance of happiness until her legs reminded her that they were still angry with her. The second message was from Sean asking her to come to his show on Friday night.

She tapped a quick affirmative to Sean's request, then thought about what she should say in response to Doug. A moment later, she typed, "I had a great time, too. Call me this evening." She debated whether she should include a smiley face, but decided that emoticons were not sexy or part of her new grownup persona.

Quinn spent the day moving at half her normal speed at work. When her uncle asked her if she was ill, she told him that she must be mentally ill for trying to fly before she could walk.

"I don't know what that means," Uncle Patrick gave her a quizzical look.

"It's a long story. Suffice it to say, I'm out of shape," Quinn replied. She had chosen a simple berry cobbler and salted caramel brownies with a whiskey sauce for the dessert choice that evening. She whisked the dry ingredients together for the cobbler.

"Yoohoo. Anyone back here?" Anne Daniels called out.

"Over here, Mom." Quinn gave her uncle a questioning look. He shook his head and mouthed a negative.

"There you are, Patrick. I tried calling your

cell phone, but it went straight to voicemail," Anne complained. She smoothed hands down her black pants and looked around the kitchen. "Looks like you've been busy this morning, darling. Is that Ma's berry cobbler recipe?"

"It is," Quinn said. "I'm trying to use as many of Grandma Rose's recipes here as possible. Comfort food."

"It certainly is. Make sure you don't taste your wares though. A minute on the lips and it's forever on the hips," Anne quoted. "Patrick, I've got the final guest list for Ma's party. I wanted to talk to you about decorations."

"Let's go into my office and talk about it so we're out of Quinn's way," Patrick steered his sister away from the bags of flour and towards his office on the other side of the kitchen.

"Sure. Quinn, you look a little tired. Are you getting enough sleep? Patrick's not working you too hard is he?"

"I went climbing yesterday, Mom. I'm a little worn out, but I'm fine."

"Why on earth would you do something like that? It's incredibly dangerous. Stick with tennis if you want a sport," Anne advised.

"Because a ball coming at your face is so much safer," Patrick said dryly. "Come on, Anne. Let's go look at your list."

Anne gave one last hard look at Quinn then followed her brother. Quinn shook her head. She thought that she would drop dead from shock if her mother ever said anything supportive. Her cell phone buzzed in her pants pocket. Wiping her floured hands on her apron, she dug it out to answer.

"Hello?"

"Quinn? It's Sean. How's tricks making the treats?"

"Good. What's up? You never call me this early on a weekday."

"Can't I just call to check on my friend? Sheesh, such a Doubting Dora." Sean clucked his tongue.

"Sean, you don't get out of bed before noon and we both know it. Spill."

"I need a favor. It's actually doing you a favor, too."

"Men are just asking me for all sorts of favors this week. Is it my perfume?" Quinn said only half in jest.

"Well, my favor means you coming to the club tonight to be a friend of mine's date."

"Why?"

"I thought you were on board with this new search for romance. I've found a nice guy who isn't a serial killer or newly released from Attica."

"I am on board. I had a great date with Doug on Sunday night and he wants to go out again. I'm even going on a pretend date with Zach tomorrow. My social calendar is so full, I may have to pencil in my Sean time for weeks in advance."

Sean sniffed. "I'm glad your school boy wasn't a total disaster, but I already told Ricardo that you would meet him at the club at eight tonight. Please, Quinnie Bear, do me this favor. He really is a nice guy and it won't be a wasted evening."

"I'll do it, but only if you tell me why it's so important I go on this date with your friend."

Sean was silent on the other end for a moment. "Okay. Here's the deal. He's actually my cousin and he knows I'm gay. He saw you and I together one day and asked me about you. He threatened to tell *Abuela* about me if I didn't set him up on a date with you. Please, Quinn," Sean begged, "say you'll do this. It would break my grandmother's heart to find out about me."

Quinn could hear the fear in Sean's voice. "Fine. I'll go out with him, but I'm taking Indie. One date. That's all," Quinn said firmly. "I'm going to be such a bitch that he'll get over his little crush on me and never want to see me again."

"Fair enough," Sean sighed in relief. "Quinn, don't be too bitchy. My Aunt Lucia is hard as nails, and Ricardo's a mama's boy. You might actually turn him on. He probably visits Dark Dreams on a weekly basis and has someone call him Ricky Boy."

"Wonderful. Thanks for the nightmare. I have to get back to work now. Call Indie and give her the rundown on the plans for tonight."

"I will," Sean said. "I really appreciate this Quinn."

Quinn disconnected. She needed to think of a way to make sure Ricardo ended this evening's date thoroughly turned off. She had to be careful though because he couldn't disclose Sean's secret. She walked to the large cooler and grabbed out a large tub of butter for her cobbler. As she measured out the scoops of butter into a large pan to melt, she had a sudden burst of inspiration. Now if she could only get Indie to agree.

That evening, Indie was sitting on a chair on Quinn's deck. "Do you really think this will work?" Indie asked. She wrinkled her nose in distaste as Quinn slowly peeled the paper away from Indie's forearm.

"It has to work. The last thing I need is Sean's creepy cousin stalking me for the rest of my life." She blew on Indie's arm. "I think it's done. Go check it out in the mirror. You look bad to the bone."

"I look like an elf with identity issues," Indie grumbled. She walked into the bathroom and flexed her bicep. The temporary tattoo Quinn had affixed to Indie's arm read, "I brake for bitches" in a circle around two women riding a motorcycle. Quinn had spent all afternoon searching bike shops and alternative stores to find the right props for the evening.

"Okay. Now you need to do mine," Quinn said. She started to loosen the tie to her yoga pants.

"Whoa!" Indie held up her hands. "Stop right there. I think you're pretty and we're good friends, but I am not touching your butt."

"I don't want you to put a tattoo on my rear

end, weirdo. How's Ricardo going to see it? I want you to put it in the small of my back. A tramp stamp."

"Oh," Indie said. "Don't I feel awkward now."

Quinn finished loosening her pants and rolled the top down so Indie could apply the tattoo. Fifteen minutes later, Quinn stood on her tiptoes looking at her butt in the mirror. In the small of her back was a tattoo of a cat arching it's back.

"How come you got the cool tattoo?" Indie complained.

"Because I'm the girl in this relationship," Quinn explained.

"You do realize how insulting that is, right?"

"I'm sorry. I get the cat in honor of Fat Panther. It kind of looks like him before he got fat and lazy."

"Fine, but you have to wear the leather fringe vest. I don't wear dead animals." Indie handed her the black fringe vest Quinn had found at Goodwill. The store had been a treasure trove of bad fashion from the eighties. Quinn felt it fit her biker chick alter ego for the evening.

She grabbed the vest and went into her room

to change. "Remember that we've been seeing each other off and on since college. Right now, we're on again. Make sure you call Ricardo's manliness into question. We want to make sure he never wants contact with me again. If we're lucky, he'll be so embarrassed that he won't want to see Sean in the foreseeable future either."

"Is it okay if I call you Sugar Britches?" Indie called.

"Whatever floats your boat, Sugar Booger," Quinn shot back. She walked out into the living room and twirled around. The fringes of the vest spun around her like brushes at an automatic car wash.

"You look like you came out of a Stevie Nicks' video," Indie said. "I like the suede boots. Nice touch."

"Who is Stevie Nicks?" Quinn asked.

"Your parents totally neglected your musical education, didn't they? What do they listen to? Opera?"

"You know what? I don't really know. They were on the road when I was little and by the time they stayed stateside, I was a teenager. Grandma Rose listened to Chubby Checkers, Elvis, Doris Day, all the popular music from the fifties and early sixties. I'm a little gray on the music of the seventies and eighties."

"You need to come to the commune. My parents have a huge album collection. They kept every record, cassette and eight track they ever bought."

"I thought living on a commune meant sharing possessions and giving up consumerism."

"They share the music with everyone else. Somehow they found a moral loophole in the commune's anti-consumer stance. Music is food for the soul according to Sunbeam, the head guru out there."

"We need to get going, Sugar Booger," Quinn said.

Indie cringed and gave Quinn a dirty look. "You and Sean better buy me breakfast this Sunday."

"You? Sean better buy both of us breakfast for the next month." Quinn locked her apartment door and started down the stairs. As luck would have it, Zach was standing on the sidewalk as they exited the building.

"Costume party?" He raised an eyebrow.

"It's a long story. We're trying to rescue Sean from being outed to Mrs. Garza and I'm rescuing Quinn from a guy with the hots for her."

"This isn't Sean's cousin, Ricardo, is it?" Zach asked, concern in his eyes.

"Yeah, it is. How did you know?" Quinn asked.

"I ran into him in the hallway the other day. He had Sean cornered. When I asked Sean about it, he blew it off. He said Ricardo threatened to tell his grandmother about what he really did for a living. I had no idea he was interested in you, Quinn. I'd be careful if I were you. He didn't seem like the kind of person you want to cross."

"I've come up with the perfect plan to make him find me utterly unappealing. Meet my biker babe, Indigo Skye. I'm her honey bunny for the evening. Look. We even got tatted up for the night." Quinn turned around and stuck her butt out slightly.

"Nice view, but please tell me those aren't real," Zach laughed.

"What?" Indie pretended to be hurt. "You don't like my biker tats? What nerve!"

"They wash off," Quinn explained. "We

wanted to make sure he believed us."

"Good luck. I'll see you tomorrow for our date, Quinn." He waved goodbye and walked into the building.

"You have a date with Zach? You didn't tell me." Indie nudged Quinn with her hip. "I thought you loved me."

"Ha ha. It's not a real date. He's trying to make his friend stop setting him up on dates. I'm his fake girlfriend."

"Ah. Like I'm your fake girlfriend."

"Exactly."

"Life was so much simpler on the commune," Indie said wistfully.

"It wasn't my idea to initiate Operation Quinnover. Now that I'm a hot dating commodity..."

"Yeah yeah. Just get in my car and let's go." Indie laughed.

CHAPTER TWENTY-THREE

http://theromancereport.blogathon.com

The Romance Report

A blog dedicated to the pursuit of love and happiness.

Tuesday, September 24, 11:28 p.m.

Happy Tuesday, dear readers! It's nice to have a date with someone that you actually like – my best friend whom I'll call Mindie, formerly known as Frenemy.

No, I haven't given up on men, but I did have to mislead a member of my stalkerazzi fan club astray. Ricky basically blackmailed me into a date. He may as well have purchased a big screaming neon sign blinking "LOSER" with an arrow at his head. I clearly had no future with Ricky. Once I met him, I saw a disturbing amount of back hair creeping out from the sides and back of his tank top (a poor fashion choice even if you do think you look like a young Sylvester Stallone.) His back was in desperate need of a depilatory. I vowed to use extreme measures to make this man lose interest in me.

Thanks to my good friend, Mindie, a plan to turn even my most avid fan into a hater was hatched. Enter Operation Quinnhatesmen. Mindie and I donned our best eighties biker chick clothes and even acquired some tastefully placed tattoos. Don't worry. They wash off with water and soap. Imagine Ricky's dismay when he saw how "in love" Mindie and I were – with each other! We were a bad clichéd stereotype, and I apologize now to my LGBT friends. If you only saw the giant hairy squirrel that was his back hair, you would understand. Being a true macho man, he decided his greasy good looks and suave ways with women would win me back to his side of the proverbial bed. He held my chair for me. He ordered my drinks for me. Mind you, he didn't ask me what I wanted to drink. He told me what I was going to drink. Do I look like a piña colada girl? Uh, no.

Due to his overbearing *machismo,* I decided Ricky needed to be put in his place – a dark cave full of other Neanderthals. Mindie somehow knew what to do. She challenged Ricky to arm wrestle. Now, those of you who don't know Mindie would think that some buff females might be able to best a man. No, dear readers, Mindie is a hundred pounds soaking wet and the size of a water sprite. She is, however, smart like a fox. She grasped Ricky's meaty hand in her dainty one and flashed him her best smile. Ricky, being a gentleman (ha!), decided to give her a chance to pin him. Mindie pretended to strain and push against his hand. Next thing our sleazy friend Ricky knew, Mindie bent across the table to reveal her amazing cleavage. Ricky was so distracted by the sight that Mindie took advantage and slammed his hand to the table. After that, his manhood was clearly in question. He huffed and puffed about letting her win. Every time he tried to put his arm around my shoulders, he would find my "girlfriend's" arm already there. She made sure she flexed her muscles every time. By the end of the night, Ricky had slunk to the bar to sit alone, and Mindie and I were able to enjoy a girl's night out in peace.

I may not have found my one true love tonight, but I did find out that true friends are rare indeed. It's nice to know that I have one willing to go the extra mile to save me from a fate worse than singlehood – a man with a big ego and a hairy back.

I bid you goodnight, dear readers, and I hope your friends are as wonderful as mine.

Comments:

Shawnalovesboys: You both are the best friends I could ever ask for. This diva owes you!. BTW, I love the cat tat on your arse!

QuinnieBee: Glad to be of service. Maybe I should make the cat tat permanent.

Dreambuilder: I don't have a hairy back.

QuinnieBee: And your point is?

CHAPTER TWENTY-FOUR

The next afternoon, Quinn hurried home from work. Exhausted from the night before, she planned to take a short nap before Zach took her to his friend's dinner party. Dating was harder work than she remembered. She slipped into a comfy pair of sweats and a camisole and slid between the sheets. Minutes later, she was fast asleep.

She awoke hours later to the sound of knocking at her door. Groggy from sleep, she yawned and looked at her bedside clock. Holy cow! It was time for her to meet up with Zach. The knock sounded on her door again. She struggled out from beneath her sheets and dashed to the door.

"Did you forget about our date?" Zach said with a disappointed glance at her bare feet and sleep-fuzzy hair.

"I'm so sorry. I fell asleep and forgot to set my alarm," Quinn apologized. "Give me twenty minutes and I'll be ready to go. There's iced tea in the fridge and a plate of stuffed mushrooms I brought home from work."

"I'm timing you," Zach joked as Quinn sprinted to the shower. Twenty-three minutes later, she emerged from her room in a dark turquoise silk shirt over slim black pants that hugged her curves. She'd pulled her damp hair into a simple chignon. A silver cuff bracelet and large silver hoop earrings completed the look.

Zach gave a low whistle. "Dang! You clean up nice."

Quinn, pleased with his response, did a little twirl as she grabbed her purse. "You ready to go?"

"I don't know if I want to share you with the rest of the world," Zach replied.

"Fake date. Remember?"

"I know. Just practicing to make us a believable couple." Zach said to her as he led Quinn to his car.

Zach's friends, Jeff and Cindy, lived in a small subdivision between Richmond and Ashland. Quinn looked around her at the cookie-cutter houses and thought she didn't ever want to live in one of these prefab boxes. She liked her brownstone and it's quirks.

"You're awfully quiet. What are you thinking about?" Zach asked as he turned down the music.

"No insult to your friends intended, but I would never want to live in suburbia," Quinn replied. "I like the hustle and bustle of the city. I like unique buildings and pipes that rumble in the winter. Walking to the corner shop and buying a coffee and a bagel gives me pleasure. If I lived out here with two kids, a fenced yard and a dog named Spot, I wouldn't be able to do those little things that make up my little world of comfort."

"I couldn't agree with you more. I grew up in one of these types of houses. It was nice having a little neighborhood of other kids to play with, but it also kept my world small. I want my kids to have access to culture and diversity, not a pre-made life. Jeff's different from me though. He grew up an Army brat so he lived in military housing and moved from base to base. He craves this kind of stability and sameness." Zach waved at the house they had pulled into and the surrounding homes.

"I can see how he could feel that way. I didn't move around, but I was shuttled back and forth between my parents' house and my Grandma Rose's. The difference is Grandma Rose's house was in the city so the city has always felt more like home to me."

The front door had a large burlap wreath hanging on it that said "Welcome." Zach rang the doorbell and a moment later, the door was opened by a tall, clean-cut man in a green polo shirt and jeans.

"What's up, man?" Jeff clapped Zach on his shoulder and motioned them inside. "You must be Quinn. You're right, Zach. She's gorgeous."

Quinn flushed a bright shade at the unexpected compliment. "Thanks."

"Honey? Is that Zach and his date?" A petite woman with a blonde bob came out drying her hands on a dish towel. "Hi! I'm Cindy. Come on into the living room and have a seat. Dinner will be ready in about twenty minutes. We've got one other couple coming, so make yourselves comfortable."

Quinn followed Zach to the large room off the front hallway. It was a comfortable room with a large screen television mounted on the wall. The walls were covered with pictures of Jeff and Cindy and what appeared to be friends and family. Quinn walked up and peered at one that had Zach in it.

He and Jeff stood at the base of a desert cliff with sunburned faces smiling at the camera.

"That was taken out in Utah. Jeff and I went climbing out there a few years ago after college," Zach said from behind her.

"I miss those days sometimes," Jeff said, "but I know climbing makes Cindy nervous, so…"

"Quinn's going to be my new climbing buddy," Zach said, placing his arm around her shoulders. "Aren't you, sweetheart?"

"I'm working on it, honey," Quinn said with a bright smile. When Jeff wasn't looking, she rolled her eyes and bared her teeth at Zach. He chuckled softly.

"So, Zach's been keeping pretty quiet about you, Quinn. How'd you two meet?" Jeff asked. Cindy walked into the room and they both gave Quinn an expectant look.

"Yes, honey, tell them how we met." Quinn smiled sweetly at him.

"It's a funny story, actually. She was on her way to a date with another guy. She ran into me and knocked me down the stairs," Zach said. He settled into an oversized chair and pulled Quinn down onto his lap.

"I barely ran into you!" Quinn sputtered.

Zach waved his finger in admonishment at her. "Who's telling the story?" Quinn crossed her arms and waited for the rest of the story.

"Anyway, as I was saying, she knocked me down the stairs. She was so embarrassed and upset that she ran to my side and held my hand until I regained consciousness. Her beautiful face was the first thing I saw when I opened my eyes. I asked her out before I even sat up. Of course, she had to say yes. It was her fault I was lying there on the ground to begin with. It was love at first sight."

Quinn stared at him open-mouthed. Although there was a small kernel of truth, she was impressed that he'd turned a small encounter into the romance of the century in just a few words.

"Ah, that's so sweet," Cindy cooed. "Quinn, you're a lucky girl. Zach's amazing."

"I'm the lucky one," Zach said and pulled Quinn to him. He kissed her lightly on the lips. Quinn felt a small tingle of electricity when his lips touched hers. She pulled back slightly and looked at him. He gave her an innocent look and turned back to Jeff and Cindy. "Quinn went climbing with me for the first time. She's pretty tough."

"I'll have to admit that I was scared, but Zach stayed right by my side until I made it to the top of the wall," Quinn said. "I felt pretty good about myself after I touched the ground again. Zach had me do something outside of my comfort zone."

"I wish Cindy would try it," Jeff said with an envious look at Zach. "I'm grounded for now."

"There's no way I'll rock climb. Too scary!" Cindy shuddered.

"It wasn't nearly as bad as I thought it would be. Zach's promised to take me to some cliffs down by the bay after I have a little more experience."

"I need to pull the chicken out of the oven," Cindy said.

"Do you need any help?" Quinn jumped up off of Zach's lap to put some distance between them.

"No. Everything's done. You just sit back down and relax." Cindy waved her back down. Zach grasped Quinn's hand and grinned at her. She scowled, but after a moment, relented and sat back down.

"So how are things going with your latest project?" Jeff asked Zach.

"Good. I found a stained glass artist whose

agreed to repair the existing windows at a reasonable price. The client's happy. I'll just be glad to put this one to bed and move on to something a little less challenging. Some of these churches are a bear to restore. Between the windows and the stonework, trying to get everything to match is exhausting. I had to fly to Vermont last week to find matching stonework."

"Quinn, what do you do?" Jeff turned to her.

"I, um, I…" What did she do? Technically, she was a journalist by training. A temporary baker?

"Quinn's got an amazing job. She's too modest to talk about it, but remember that restaurant we went to when you and Cindy came into town last time?"

"Hanrahan's? Yeah. I love that place."

"Quinn's one of the chefs there," Zach bragged.

"Well, honey, don't exaggerate. I just make the desserts."

"Her desserts are good enough to get the newspaper to mention them," Zach added. "She's promised to teach me how to cook."

"Good luck with that," Jeff laughed. "He

can't even cook hot dogs without burning them. Don't tell Cindy you're a chef. She's a great cook, but she's always nervous that something will taste wrong or people won't like her cooking."

"Mum's the word." Quinn pretended to turn a lock on her mouth. "My Uncle Patrick owns Hanrahan's. I'm not a trained chef."

"Not yet," Zach said, "but if you go to culinary school, there won't be a restaurant in the country that won't be beating down your door to hire you."

Quinn felt awkward that Zach had so much faith in her abilities. Of course, he was probably just saying it to impress his friends. After all, wasn't that what she was there to do. Impress them so they would think he wasn't single and looking for love?

The doorbell rang and Jeff excused himself to answer it. Quinn leapt off Zach's lap and turned to him. "I know I agreed to throw your friends off the scent, but cool it to a simmer rather than a boil?"

"Sorry." Zach gave her a sheepish look. "You are an amazing chef, though."

"How would you know? I haven't even started your cooking lessons yet."

"I've been eating at your uncle's restaurant

since you started there," Zach admitted. "I've got to eat somewhere and between you and your uncle, it's the best food in town. Your chocolate orange cake thing is my favorite dessert so far."

Quinn stood staring at him for a minute then burst out laughing. "If I knew you liked the food there so much, I could have saved you the trouble and just brought things home with me."

"I didn't want you to think I was weird or anything," Zach wouldn't meet her eyes. "I really can't cook."

"It's okay, Zach," Quinn walked back over to him. She scooched him over on the chair and sat next to him. "It's kind of sweet that you stalk my cooking."

"It is?" Zach looked up at her expectantly.

"It is," Quinn conceded. "It's kind of flattering. I'm still debating on whether I should go to school like my uncle offered."

"I think you should. I'll have to move to another city if you do, but you definitely should."

Quinn looked at him, confused. "Why would you need to move?"

"Because if you get any better, I'll weigh five hundred pounds. I'd have to move away to keep from eating at your restaurant every night!"

CHAPTER TWENTY-FIVE

http://theromancereport.blogathon.com

The Romance Report

A blog dedicated to the pursuit of love and happiness.

Thursday, September 26, 7:49 p.m.

It's a distinctly different Thursday here at The Romance Report headquarters. My friend, Shawna, believed that I was living under a curse. In her mind, this curse was sapping my love life and my luck. The cure? A visit to the local *curandera*. For those of you dear readers not familiar with the term, it is the Spanish word for healer. Yes, that's correct, dear readers, I went to a healer to have my unlucky in love curse removed.

I know what you are all thinking, Quinn's lost her ever loving mind! But I beg to differ. Let me describe the evening to you and maybe you will change your mind.

Shawna picked me up in her sassy Mini Cooper that I love to ride in with her. We zipped through traffic until we arrived at our destination. I was momentarily taken aback by the location. It wasn't a house. It wasn't a hut high on a mountain top. Nope. It was a neon-signed storefront in a strip mall with a K-Mart next door. Healings are now twenty-first century and commercialized.

Shawna's cousin, Angie, met us at the door since we arrived after hours. No turban. No crystal balls. Just a front desk with a small room behind it with chairs and something like a doctor's examining table covered by a sheet. She did have one corner with candles, cups, fruit and feathers, but I didn't pay that close attention. Now I wish I had because it's fascinating!

As soon as I walked in, she said she could sense a heavy burden on me. She told me that I was at a crossroads. Was she an intuitive woman or did Shawna spill the beans about me beforehand? I'll never know for sure, but Shawna swears she didn't tell her anything besides my name and that I was suffering from bad luck.

Angie had me sit down and she sat opposite of me. She asked me a few questions about my health. She asked me what brought me to see her and I told her about all of the bad luck I had with men and with my job. She held both my hands while we spoke. I might have imagined it, but I a warmth spread from her hands into mine and into my arms. As we spoke, a sense of calmness settled over me.

When we were done, Angie said she would perform a *limpia* or cleansing. She had me lie on the table. I heard her say a few words of prayer in Spanish and she lit a candle. Then she picked up an egg and sprinkled some water from a glass container on it. She started at the top of my head and skimmed it downward over every part of my body while saying words I didn't understand (hopefully, it was for luck and love). It was weird. I felt incredibly awkward as she cleansed me with an egg. To be honest, dear readers, I almost jumped up and ran out of the building.

After she was done rubbing the egg all over me like a bar of soap. She cracked the egg into a bowl filled with water and had me come look at it with her. It didn't really float, and it didn't really sink. My egg was wishy-washy (kind of like I've been feeling myself lately.) It also had some weblike things coming from the yolk. Angie said I was trapped at this point in my life due to something holding me back. Angie felt like it was due to my own self-doubt. (Great! Like I didn't already know I was filled with doubts…sheesh!)

She had me sit back down next to her. She said that my bad luck in love was not due to outside forces, but my own lack of self-worth. My spirit was ill. She said I had to know my own value before anyone else could value me. She could have been channeling Grandma Rose because she said the same thing to me! Angie said that the *limpia* should have removed the bad luck or *mal de ojo,* but if I continued to have problems to back and see her.

Here's the odd thing. Before I left, she grabbed ahold of my hand and said that she had a vision of me with lightning or electricity all around me and a man whose face she couldn't see (dang it!) She wasn't one hundred percent sure, but she believed that my true love would have electricity with me. Weird.

Anyway, dear readers, this ends my tale of cleansing by egg. I'm not sure I'm a believer, but I'm also a person who is starting to believe that anything is possible.

Comments:

Shawnalovesboys: Glad you got cleansed, girlfriend. You never know when someone has given you the evil eye. Maybe an ex?

QuinnieBee: My exes don't have enough gumption to bother with cursing me.

Chica411: My grandma was an old-school *curandera* and I'm a believer. I promise that you will see a change in your life. Just make sure you go back and see her if it doesn't. You might need to be uncrossed.

QuinnieBee: I did feel some kind of energy that I couldn't quite put my finger on when I was there. I'll keep you updated via The Romance Report if it works!

Dreambuilder: I think you're already making your own luck. Believe in yourself and anything is possible.

QuinnieBee: I think you're right! I plan to start living my life with or without a man. If the right guy comes along, I'll know he's the one when he remembers how I drink my coffee and doesn't mind my love of B-grade horror films.

Dreambuilder: Good to know.

CHAPTER TWENTY-SIX

"Your grandmother's birthday party is next weekend," Quinn's mother said. "I sent out invitations yesterday. I need you to come shopping with me for her present today."

"I can't. I have a date with Doug this afternoon," Quinn said. She carefully applied polish to her toes. She wiggled them. Bright blue was actually pretty on toes. She should have ventured beyond shell pink a long time ago.

"He can meet you downtown and pick you up after you're done shopping. We can have lunch."

"Mother, I don't want to ask Doug to come downtown. It's only our second date."

"Fine. Where are you two planning to go? We can shop in the nearby stores. The party is a week away and I have to be in D.C. all next week. This is our last chance to buy a family gift for Ma."

Quinn sighed. She wasn't going to win this

battle, so she might as well wave the white flag. "Fine. I'll have Doug meet us. We're going to the movies at Short Pump."

"Perfect! I like the shops there better than downtown anyway. He can pick you up at three o'clock. I'll be there at eleven to get you." She disconnected before Quinn could respond.

"Sure, Mom. Whatever you say, Mom. Change my day's plans, Mother. Augh!" Quinn shouted to her empty apartment. Fat Panther, startled by the loud sound, jumped down and hid underneath her couch.

Quinn dialed Doug's number. "Hi, Doug. It's Quinn. I'm calling about our date this afternoon."

"You're not calling to cancel are you?" Doug sounded disappointed.

"No! It's just that my mother wants me to go shopping for my Grandma Rose's birthday present. Can you meet me at the theater rather than pick me up here at my apartment?"

"That's not a problem at all. It will give me a chance to meet your mom," Doug said.

"I wouldn't get too excited. My mother can be a little…how can I say this without scaring you…interrogating."

"She's a reporter, isn't she? I wouldn't expect anything else. I'll prepare my best sound bites for her report."

"You're the best. I'll see you at three?"

"On the dot. Bye."

Quinn tossed the cell phone on the coffee table and finished polishing her toenails. Pleased with the look, she hobbled into the kitchen to pour herself another cup of coffee. She and Indie had gone to Hello! Sailor to watch Sean's latest show. Quinn still hadn't figured out how someone with Sean's masculine good looks transformed into a gorgeous woman four nights a week. He could sing, too. Quinn hummed one of Shawna's tunes from the night before.

"Hey, big spender, spend a little time with me." Quinn gave a high kick with one leg like a Vegas showgirl. Unfortunately, she overshot and lost her balance. She landed with a loud thump on her butt and sent her into paroxysms of laughter. "Fat Panther, you think I'd better stick with the day job?"

A moment later, she heard a loud knock on her door. "Quinn, you okay? I heard something crash."

"I'm okay, Zach," Quinn called out from her spot on the floor. "Give me a second."

Quinn got up from her spot on the floor. Thank goodness her toes were still perfect. She hobbled to the door. "Hey, Zach. Come on in." She wiped the tears of laughter from her eyes.

"Are you okay? Are you hurt?" He grasped her arm and checked her over from head to toe, concern in his eyes.

"I'm fine. A klutz, but fine. I'm laughing, not crying." Quinn hiccupped.

"Thank goodness. I was worried for a second." Zach wore a pair of ripped blue jeans spattered with different colors of paint and an old faded black t-shirt. "I was coming up to see you anyway. I promised to paint your bathroom. Is today okay?"

"You don't mind doing it while I'm not here, do you? I have to go shopping with my mother, then I have a date with Doug."

"Doug? Is that the college friend?"

"Yes. We're off to the movies this afternoon," Quinn said. She felt a little self-conscious talking to Zach about Doug and she wasn't exactly sure why.

"Second date?"

"Yep. You're okay painting the bathroom today?" Quinn asked, changing the subject.

"Point me to a paintbrush and I'll get started," Zach said with more enthusiasm than Quinn could ever muster for household improvement projects.

"I have everything right there." She pointed to the can of paint, roller and brush stashed in her living room corner.

Zach picked up the paint supplies while Quinn tidied up her pedicure tools. No guy wanted to see a pumice stone and toenail clippers on a girl's living room floor. She stashed them in her basket of clothes she had folded that morning and carried it all into her bedroom.

"I like the color you painted your bedroom walls," Zach said behind her.

Quinn jumped a foot into the air from surprise. "Holy cow! Don't sneak up on me like that! I nearly had a heart attack."

"A heart attack at your age is unlikely," Zach joked. "I'm glad you're moving away from the zebra austerity phase of decorating. These colors suit your personality better. What about the kitchen?"

"I was thinking about a dark blue or wine shade. I still haven't decided."

"I think dark blue would look great with your cabinets," Zach said. "I did one class in interior decorating so that I could help clients who restored historical homes with their interiors as well."

"You are an interesting man, Zach Taylor." Quinn gave him an appraising look. "I got lucky when you moved into the building."

"I'm glad you think so. Let me get started. I'll have your bathroom done before you get back from your date."

"I need to run downstairs and give Mrs. Garza my check for rent. I'll be back in a few minutes," Quinn said. She slipped on her shoes and grabbed her checkbook.

"Go ahead. I'll be busy taping," Zach said in a distracted voice. He was already setting up to paint.

Quinn headed to Mrs. Garza. She knocked on her landlady's door. Sean answered, his eyes red and swollen. "What's wrong? Are you okay?" Quinn asked him.

"I'm screwed six days to Sunday," Sean

wailed. He turned and left the door open for Quinn to follow him,

"Nothing can be that bad," Quinn said. She closed the door behind her and followed Sean into the living room where he sat with tears in his eyes.

"Yes it can. Ricardo told *abuela* about me. He came this morning and woke her up. I walked into the kitchen as he described my current job in detail to her."

"What did she do?" Quinn asked. She couldn't imagine being in Sean's shoes right now. His grandmother was old-fashioned and very devout in her faith.

"She got up, told Ricardo she would talk to him later and got ready for Mass like she always does. She didn't speak one word to me," Sean sobbed. "She's never going to forgive me and my family will disown me."

"Oh, Sean! I'm so sorry." Quinn sat down on the couch and wrapped her arms around him. His shoulders shook as he quietly cried.

Quinn heard a key rattle in the door and a moment later, Reyna Garza walked into the living room. When she saw Sean crying, concern filled her eyes and she rushed over to the couch. *"M'hijo!*

What's wrong? Are you hurt?"

Sean looked up at his grandmother. "I broke your heart. I'm not the good grandson you thought I was."

"Really? When I fell and needed someone to take me back and forth to physical therapy three times a week, who took me?"

"I did," Sean responded in a small voice.

"When I was scared to stay on my own anymore, who gave up their privacy and their own place to come stay with a foolish old woman?"

"Me, but you aren't foolish…"

"Don't interrupt. I am a foolish old woman because I've known all along and I let you continue with this charade."

"What? You knew? How come you didn't say anything?" Sean asked, his tears drying up.

"Because you didn't want me to know, so I thought you were ashamed. Ashamed of your heritage, ashamed of who you are. You're young and I knew eventually you would work through it and come to realize what I've known all along."

"What?" Quinn said. "Oops. Sorry. I got caught up in the moment."

Quinn's interruption caused Sean and Mrs.

Garza to both laugh.

"Yes, what?" Sean sniffled.

"I know that you are a handsome gay Mexican man who loves his family and his friends. I'm proud of you, Juan Carlos. You need to be proud of who you are and quit hiding your authentic self. Ricardo has always had *mamitis aguda,* and everyone knows it."

"He is definitely a mama's boy. You still love me? You're not ashamed of me?" Sean asked. Quinn could see he still held back as if he still didn't believe his grandmother would accept him.

"Of course I still love you." She sat down on the other side of Sean. "I loved you from the moment your mother brought you and your brother Julian home from the hospital, *mi principito.*"

Sean sniffled then kissed his grandmother on her wrinkled cheek. "I was so worried that I'd broken your heart. I would have told you years ago, but I was ashamed of who I was. I mean, I love being Shawna on stage because it's the only time I feel that I'm being me."

"You be proud of all of you. Juan Carlos, Sean and Shawna. I may not agree with all of your choices, but I will stand by your side as long as you are honest and a good person," Mrs. Garza said. She squeezed Sean's hand then turned to Quinn. "Young lady, when are you going to start being true to yourself. I see you dating these mala personas…bad guys. You wear another person's face to please the world when you need to realize that you are fine just being Quinn Daniels."

"I'm trying, Mrs. Garza," Quinn stammered, "but it's hard with family…"

"Your family's a whole lot easier to deal with than mine!" Sean interrupted her. "Try being Mexican and gay in my family then come crying to me about your mother."

"I'm trying. Baby steps, Sean. I'm taking baby steps, but soon I'll be ready to take that giant leap for Quinnkind," Quinn joked, trying to lighten the mood. "Oh crap! I better get upstairs. My mother's probably already here and Zach's in my apartment painting."

"Zach is a good man," Reyna Garza said. "He is a man who lives his life the way he wants to live it. Honesty in a man is a good quality. You could do worse."

"I…he…uh…he and I are friends," Quinn

finished weakly. "Here's my rent check. I'd better get going." Quinn thrust her check into Sean's hands and darted out of the apartment before they probed and pushed her anymore.

She flew up the stairs. She reached to open her apartment door, but she stopped when she heard her mother's laugh. Steeling her nerves, she turned the doorknob and walked inside to see her mother sitting at her kitchen table with a cup of coffee, and Zach sitting opposite her.

"Honey, there you are. I was getting ready to send out a search party, but Zach said he would call in the Mounties and handle it," Anne said then proceeded to giggle like a schoolgirl.

"Anne, I keep a close eye on Quinn," Zach said.

"Quinn, you didn't tell me your new neighbor was so charming," Anne admonished her. "I'll sit here and finish my coffee while you get changed."

"I wasn't going to change. I'm wearing this," Quinn said. She wore her favorite pair of indigo blue jeans with a long-sleeved cream t-shirt and a deep blue scarf tied the look together.

"You're awfully casual for a date," Anne

said, casting a critical eye over Quinn's clothes, "but if you're ready, let's get going. Zach, it was a pleasure to meet you."

Zach grasped Anne's outstretched hand. "It was such an honor to meet you. I've been reading your news stories for years. I'll see you at the party next weekend."

Quinn shook her head, not sure she'd heard hi correctly. Her mother had been viciously slashing the guest list to make sure they stayed under seventy-five guests, yet she clearly had invited Zach to the party. "You're coming to Grandma Rose's party?"

"Your mother invited me. I'm excited to meet your uncle. I told your mother I eat at Hanrahan's at least once a week."

"Quinn, why don't you have Zach bring you to Ma's party? You know I worry about you driving that wreck of a car of yours and you don't want to take the bus in a nice dress and heels."

"We'll see. Let's get going." Quinn grabbed her purse and tried to herd her mother towards the door. "Zach, thanks for painting my bathroom. I appreciate it."

"See you later. Have fun at the movies,"

Zach called after her.

Anne drove them to the stores near Short Pump. Quinn and her mother zipped from store to store looking for the perfect present. They finally found the perfect gift at a small jewelry store with an in-store jeweler. He helped them pick out a ring which would hold Grandma Rose's birthstone surrounded by smaller stones with Anne's, Patrick's and Quinn's different birthstones. The setting would be white gold. Fortunately, Anne and her mother wore the same size ring, so the jeweler could size it correctly. Anne paid for it and the jeweler promised it would be ready the day before the party.

"Whew! My feet are killing me," Quinn's mom said, "and I'm starving. Why don't we hit the little bistro we like near the theater and then I can take you to meet your date."

"His name is Doug," Quinn said. Her mother had a great memory for names, so she knew it was a deliberate oversight. "Sure. They have a great portabella mushroom sandwich."

Quinn and her mom ordered lunch. They were enjoying an appetizer of spinach and artichoke dip with pita chips when Quinn's phone pinged to notify her that she had a text. It was Indie.

"I need you to go on a date with Marty and me. He has a friend who tries to tag along and hang out with us wherever we go. You have to go with us to this festival so he's not a third wheel. You owe me."

Quinn typed back. "Ugh. Okay. I'll do it. When?"

"Friday night."

"Fine. I have Grandma's birthday that weekend so I can beg out early if I need too."

"Okay. Will call you tomorrow to confirm."

Anne harrumphed quietly across from Quinn. "Sorry, Mom. It was Indie. She needed me to help her out with something."

"How is Indigo? I haven't seen her in months."

"She's great. She has a new boyfriend, Marty, who works at an insurance company. She wants me to meet him next weekend."

"If Indie can find a man with a normal job, surely you can, Quinn," Anne said. "Indie and Sean are on the invitation list for next week. They should have received their invitations. Please make sure to remind them to RSVP so I can confirm numbers with your uncle for the food."

"Yes, ma'am," Quinn mumbled. She took a bite of her sandwich to keep from saying anything else.

"So remind me what your date does for a living? I couldn't remember what you told me."

"Doug's a middle school teacher, Mother. I went to college with him. We were friends. Actually, more like acquaintances, but he's a nice guy."

"A middle school teacher." Anne nodded thoughtfully. "It's a respectable profession. Tough working with middle school children. I have to admire his courage. Plus, a number of teachers eventually move into administration. He could become principal of a school one day or even superintendent if he plans well."

"It's fairly early in his career for him to plan on taking over the school board," Quinn said dryly.

"It's never too early to plan for your future, particularly when it comes to you career. I knew what I wanted when I was in high school. I had a full life plan when I graduated including career, marriage and children. I haven't veered from that plan and look at my successes," Anne said. She pointed her fork at Quinn and said, "You need to get your life plan together. No more flitting from job to job or man to man. Pick a path and stick with it and you will be successful."

"I don't flit from job to job. I've had two jobs, not counting the one with Uncle Pat. I've had three serious boyfriends. I'm figuring it out, Mother. Give me a break," Quinn said.

She pushed her plate away from her. She had lost her appetite. Her mother was never happy with her men, her job, her clothes or well, pretty much anything she did. Quinn didn't know why she kept on trying to please her mother. If Quinn's plans didn't fit into Anne Daniel's "life plan" then they didn't qualify as important. She checked the time.

"I need to go if I'm going to meet Doug. It's only a block away. Finish your lunch and I'll walk over there."

"Don't be silly. Call Doug and tell him you'll be a few minutes late. I'm sure he'll understand."

"It's okay," Quinn said. She flagged down their waiter and handed him her credit card to pay the bill. "Lunch is on me, Mother."

"I planned on paying for lunch, dear. I know

you've probably been strapped for cash working for my brother. I'm surprised you have money for food."

"It's fine. I'm fine. My food situation is fine," Quinn said. She signed her name to the credit card slip with an angry flourish and stood up to leave. "I'll see you at Grandma's party next week. Bye."

"Okay," Anne said, confused by Quinn's sudden coldness. "See you later."

Quinn strode away and left the restaurant before she lost her temper. Breathe, Quinn. It will be okay. You've dealt with your mother's bossiness for years. Why is it getting to you now?

"Quinn?"

She looked up and was startled to see Doug standing in front of her. "Oh, hi."

"You okay? You walked right past me. I had to jog to get in front of you."

"I'm sorry. My mother has a tendency to spin me up and make me out of sorts," Quinn said. She smiled at Doug, "but I'm sure spending time with you and watching the movie will put me in a better mood."

"*Chains of Gory* is an odd film to put you into a better mood, but okay," Doug said. "I'm not an aficionado of bad horror flicks so I bow to your better judgment."

"B-rated horror films are the best. You get the thrill without the chill because you're generally laughing too hard at the bad acting."

Doug paid for their tickets, and they grabbed a small tub of popcorn and two sodas. As they settled into their seats, Doug said, "If you ever need to vent about anything, I'm happy to listen. After middle school girl drama all day, I'm sure yours is mild in comparison. I don't scare easily, and I'm a good listener."

"Ah, that's sweet. I'm okay though. My mother never fails to disappoint with her constant barrage of criticism. She means well, and I usually ignore it," Quinn said.

The lights dimmed, and the advertisements and previews began. Soon the theater was filled with the sounds of squeals and giggles as a masked man inflicted terror on a remote private school in the mountains. At one point in the movie, Quinn jumped and Doug put his arm around her shoulders. Quinn moved closer and smiled. Their hands brushed in the popcorn tub and lingered for a moment. Two scream-laden hours later, they left the theater holding hands.

Doug drove Quinn back to her brownstone. Quinn knew he expected to be asked up, but for some reason, she didn't feel ready. He walked her to the front step and as she said her farewell, he pulled her to him and kissed her.

"I'll call you tomorrow," Doug said and gave her a gentle chuck under her chin.

"Bye," Quinn said softly. She walked slowly inside. Nothing. He kissed her, and she felt absolutely nothing. No tingle. No spark. Zip. She climbed her stairs and as she passed Zach's apartment, she lingered for a minute. She went to knock on his door but stopped. She walked up the third flight of stairs and into her apartment.

When she unlocked the door, she had to stop and make sure she was in the right location. Zach had painted her bathroom and somehow had managed to paint her small kitchen an amazing shade of blue. She looked around her apartment. Wait a minute. There were some framed photographs on her living room wall that weren't there when she left. She dropped her purse on the floor and wandered inside to look.

"Do you like it?"

Quinn let out a small scream and jumped. She turned around and saw Zach, Sean and Indie standing in her doorway.

"What's going on here?" Quinn asked.

"We did your apartment while you were gone. Zach came and grabbed me as soon as you left. I called Indie and sent her on a mission for paint. I told her Indigo Sky Blue. Get it?" Sean waited for Quinn's response.

"I'm overwhelmed. I…" Quinn stuttered. She looked at the living room walls closer and realized they were painted a pale shade of blue that complemented the dark blue of the kitchen. She peered at the framed photographs hanging on the wall. They were a series of photos showing a butterfly emerging from a chrysalis.

"I love it!" Quinn exclaimed. "I absolutely, positively love it."

"Good," Indie said as the three of them finally felt brave enough to enter the apartment, "because I was dreading the cover-up paint job on the kitchen. Dark blue is a bear to cover."

"Zach, I can't believe you pulled this off," Quinn said. "I've only been gone a few hours."

"The minute you walked out the door I was

on it. I am a man with a plan and you have the friends to help me do it."

"Where did you guys get the photographs?" Quinn asked.

"My mom took those at the commune. It's part of a series of nature pictures she did last year. Consider them an early birthday present," Indie said. She led Quinn towards her couch. "Look. I sewed you some pillows, too. Aren't they cool?"

"You sew?" Quinn was surprised. Indie never struck her as a crafty girl.

"This surprises you? I grew up on a commune where they reused everything. I have dresses made from old underwear."

"Girl, I need to get some of those for my next act." Sean whistled. "I'd be the hottest diva in town if I wore undie dresses. Oh, that could a line of clothing. Picture it. Shawna's Unhidden Undies. Shawna's Panty Pants. Shawna's…"

"Alright! We get it!" Quinn protested with a laugh.

"How did your date with Doug go?" Indie asked.

"I better get going," Zach interrupted. "I have to drive down to Abingdon early tomorrow morning to look at a home in the historic district that is having some issues. Quinn, I'm glad you like it. Go check out your bathroom." He gave her a wink and left.

"So, how did the date go?" Sean prompted.

"It was…" Quinn hesitated, "nice."

"Nice? That's what I call dinner with a friend, not a future lover," Sean said.

"He kissed me and it was just…nice."

"Uh oh," Indie said. "Sean, open a bottle of wine, stat!" She pulled Quinn down to sit on the couch.

"I don't know what's wrong with me. I meet a nice guy who has a normal job and takes me on a date and actually pays. There was no spark. No bedazzle. Just a plain, boring kiss." Quinn slumped dejectedly on her new pillows. "I'm a glutton for losers. Please let me become a nun."

"No. A. You aren't Catholic. B. You have given up black and white as wardrobe choices and finally, oh hell no, I didn't do my best work on your hair and brows for you to throw it all away!" Sean snapped his fingers at her. "You just need a guy who has some sex appeal and a…"

"Sean!" Indie squealed.

"Oh my god. I was going to say job. You girls are killing me. You two make me want to be a straight man," Sean complained.

"Heaven forbid that day should ever come. Every girl needs a gay friend with better taste in clothes than her," Indie said. "Where's our wine, Diva?"

"It's coming. Hold on to your big girl panties."

"I don't have to become a nun. I could work and hang out with you two. I don't need a man in my life to be complete," Quinn said and let out a little wail of distress. "I'm a three-time love loser. Wait. Four. Creepy Fifty Shades of Yuck dude. Criminal Creeper. Ricardo the Orangutan and now, Doug."

"There's hope for you yet. You're going out with Josh on Friday, remember?"

"Who's Josh?" Sean asked as he handed them their glasses of wine.

"It's a friend of Marty's. We're going to a comic book convention on Friday. Quinn's coming along as Josh's date."

"A comic book festival? Why?" Sean wrinkled his nose is distaste.

"I happen to like graphic novels and comic books," Indie protested. "They aren't the same as they used to be when we were kids. Much better story lines. Women are not just half-naked sex symbols nowadays."

"Thank goodness. Nobody wants to see that!" Sean exclaimed. "Give me Wolverine in a tight suit that shows off his…"

"Sean!" Quinn gasped.

"Muscles, dirty girl. I was going to say muscles. Why do you two always assume I have sex on the brain. I am a complex person with depths you two don't realize."

"Fine. You have depth. Use your deepness to figure out why I can't date a decent guy."

"I'm taking you back to Angie."

"No. I think it's more than a cleansing can cure. It's something wrong with me. Not a curse."

"You need to date Zach." Sean informed her.

"What? No. He's my friend and my neighbor. If it all goes to hell in the proverbial handbasket, I would have to move and I have this great apartment that's all colorful and stuff." Quinn waved her hands around at her various new decorations and painted walls. "I like living here."

"I don't think it would go south. Zach's a decent guy. He's hot. He's got a job. A real job. He likes you. What's not to love about him?"

"He's too busy for a relationship right now," Quinn protested. "He's got his own business that keeps him on the road. He doesn't have time for a relationship."

"A. He would make time. B. He has his own business which means he's successful and has his crap together. C. Quit being scared of anything that might be genuine." Sean ticked off the list on his fingers.

"Are we going to work our way through the alphabet tonight?" Quinn grumbled and took a sip of her wine.

"No, but we are going to have a glass of wine and a long talk about what you really want in life," Indie said. "Sean, fill 'er up. It's going to be a long night."

CHAPTER TWENTY-SEVEN

Quinn did not want to get up the next morning when she turned off her alarm. It was way too early for a girl who had finished a bottle of wine on her own. She blamed Sean. He kept refilling her glass. She slunk her way into the bathroom and peered in the mirror.

"Holy cow. I look bad," Quinn said to her reflection. She looked around her bathroom. Zach had done a nice job on the paint. She saw a small package sitting on the edge of the tub she hadn't noticed the night before in her wine-induced haze. She picked it up and saw it had a small card attached. She opened it up and read the little notecard.

"Quinn, I thought you might appreciate these after our next climbing adventure. Also, every girl should have a hot pink carabiner to use when climbing." Quinn smiled. Inside the package was a box of lavender-scented Epsom salts and a pink carabiner.

She made her way to her kitchen. She really did like the dark blue paint Indie had chosen. Fixing herself a cup of coffee, she sat down on her couch and waited for the coffee to kick in and wake her up. She had made a decision sometime last night while talking to Sean and Indie. She would go to culinary school. Cooking and baking made her happy. If she could make a living doing it, why not? If it failed, she could always fall back on journalism, but right now, she had to take a shot.

She sat drinking her coffee while she considered her decision. She would have to ask Uncle Patrick if she could still work for him as a hostess or something. She needed to pay her rent still and allowing him to do so was out of the question. She finished her coffee and got ready for work.

Quinn moved slow when she first arrived at the restaurant. Although she didn't have a headache, she did have wine fog dulling her senses. Soon, she was mixing ingredients for rolls and considering what apple-based dessert she should make. Fall was in the air, and Quinn was excited about all the things she could make with apples and pumpkin.

"So what's my favorite niece up to this morning?" Uncle Patrick's voice boomed, pulling Quinn from her reverie.

"Nothing much. I'm trying to decide what to make with all these apples. An apple crisp or apple dumplings with a vanilla ice cream side?"

"Why not both and then a brownie for folks that don't care for apples?" Uncle Patrick suggested.

"Good idea. That's what I'll do," Quinn said. She hesitated and then screwing up her courage she blurted, "I'd like to go to culinary school, but I need to keep working here at least part-time to pay my rent."

Uncle Patrick stepped back in surprise. "Really?"

"Yes. I love doing all this." Quinn motioned around the kitchen. "Is the offer for you to help still there?"

Instead of answering, Uncle Patrick pulled her into a big bear hug. "I'm proud of you. I know this isn't an easy decision for you to make. I needed to talk to you about the job today anyway."

Quinn pulled back from him. "It's about time

for Jenny to come back. Time's flown by and I hadn't even realized."

"Yes and no. Her leg is healed, but she's pregnant. She and her husband decided that she's going to stay home for the duration. Once the baby's born, she wanted to go to part-time. How do you feel about splitting the job with her?"

"Are you serious?" Quinn grinned. "It's perfect. I can start my classes and still be able to pay my rent. Thank you!"

"I'll talk to my friend at the school. We'll fill out the paperwork and get the ball rolling this afternoon. In the meantime, I see some apples waiting to be peeled."

"Aye aye, cap'n!" Quinn saluted her uncle and turned back to her bread dough. She was excited, but nervous about her decision to return to school. She had to figure out a way to break the news to her parents. On that somber thought, she started to peel apples.

The week passed quickly. Quinn submitted her paperwork to go to culinary school. Doug had called to ask for a date for the upcoming weekend. Quinn explained that she had plans with Indie and her grandmother's birthday party.

"Okay," Doug said, disappointment filling his voice. Well, maybe we can do something the following week. This week was bad for me anyway. We have parent teacher conferences. It's my least favorite part of the job."

"I don't think anyone likes them. Teachers, parents or the kids," Quinn said. She liked Doug, but after their kiss fizzled on Sunday, she wasn't sure she wanted to invest in a relationship with him. She might go on one more date to make sure there was no chemistry.

Friday arrived and Quinn realized she had no idea what to wear to a comic book convention. Indie was going to pick her up at five o'clock. She decided on an off-white blouse paired with black jodhpur pants and boots. She felt like she should be riding a horse but believed it would work for a comic festival. It made her feel a little like a superhero.

Indie texted to say she would be out front to pick her up in five minutes. Quinn flicked her brush through her hair one last time and headed downstairs to meet her.

Indie pulled up in Herbie. Quinn peered into the car, but she didn't see anyone else. "Where are our dates?"

"We're meeting them at Marty's place and then switching cars to head over together. Marty had a meeting today that ran late, so I said we would meet them. I like the outfit. Where's your faithful steed?"

"Hardy har har har. You are so funny."

"You look cute. You know I'm only yanking your chain."

Indie zipped in and out of rush hour traffic and fifteen minutes later, they were pulling up to a small house in an older residential area on the outskirts of the city. Quinn got out of the car and followed Indie to the house. She knocked on the door and moments later it was opened by a masked man.

CHAPTER TWENTY-EIGHT

http://theromancereport.blogathon.com

The Romance Report

A blog dedicated to the pursuit of love and happiness.

Friday, October 5, 8:18 p.m.

It has been an interesting evening, dear readers. I promised Mindie I would go on a double date since I owed her after our Ric the hairy-backed beast debacle. Imagine my surprise when I met my date, and he was wearing tights and a mask.

I know what you're thinking, dear readers. It was a repeat of my date at Dark Dreams, but nothing could be farther from the truth. My date was a comic book geek. He had created his very own superhero costume. He was Super Dork. He thought he was clever, but I thought it was accurate.

He had covered his chubby frame in a garish

yellow spandex costume with a large green "G" on his chest. His face was covered by a matching mask. He removed it when we were first introduced, but I quickly asked him to put it back on. Yes, dear readers, it was that bad. Mindie may have to go back to frenemy status.

Determined to make the best of my evening, I cheerfully embarked on my first foray into the comic world. At least that part of the date was interesting and I had fun. I never read comic books or manga as a kid, but the quality and variety is amazing. I also met some unique individuals at the festival.

I begged off extending my blind (or should I say masked) date to include dinner. Super Dork was a heavy mouth breather. I spent the whole evening looking over my shoulder waiting to see a pack of hounds running me down.

As Frenemy and her cronies dropped me off at my apartment, Super Dork leaned over and panted, "Do you want to feel what's under my tights?"

I punched him in the nose.

Comments:

IndigoRainbowUnicorn: I love you, my friend. Please take me off Frenemy status. At least, Super Dork won't be trailing along on my dates with M. anymore.

QuinnieBee: Apologies to M. I feel bad for losing my temper, but I'm done with dating. The tights were the fashion faux pas that broke this camel's back. M. was super nice. Definitely need to spend time with him without the Breather.

IndigoRainbowUnicorn: Will do. M. liked you, too.

Dreambuilder: Glad you didn't find your soulmate in those tights. Did you like the gift I left you? Hot pink is a good color.

QuinnieBee: OMG! It's you! I loved it. It was the perfect gift. Thank you.

CHAPTER TWENTY-NINE

Quinn had begged for Sean's help getting ready for her grandmother's birthday party. "Come on, Sean. You know I can't do my eyebrows and hair," Quinn begged. "Please? Pretty please with brown sugar and sunshine on top?"

"Honey, the only brown sugar in here is me. I will do your hair, but only if you let me pick out a dress for you. I don't want to waste all of my amazing talent just for you to drag out that yesterday's news dress you always wear."

"It's an expensive black dress. My mother gave it to me," Quinn protested.

"You do this on my terms or no Diva Shawna Makeover in your future."

"Fine," Quinn said, relenting.

Now she sat perched in her living room on a chair with her hair in large rollers. Sean gave her eyebrows a critical look. "I showed you how to shape your brows. Why aren't you shaping your brows?"

"Who has time? I jump out of bed, shower and go. Bread to bake. Pies to roll."

"There is no excuse for poor eyebrow maintenance." Sean clucked his disapproval and began to tweeze Quinn's brow. "I'm going to do this one more time, but after this, I expect you to do this once a week. *Comprende*?"

"Yes, sir," Quinn said meekly. "Ouch!"

"Beauty is pain. Pain is beauty."

"Did you get that out of a fortune cookie?" Indie asked, popping her head up from her computer. Beside her, Marty chuckled. Marty had turned out to be a great guy. Funny, smart, handsome in a nerdy sort of way, and he was very sweet to Indie. He didn't say much, but his silence was a nice balance to Indie's louder ways.

"Open your eyes so I can put some liner on them." Sean commanded Indie as he dug through his box of eye pencils and brushes.

Twenty minutes later, Sean announced his newest masterpiece was finished except for the dress. "You have to keep your eyes closed."

"How am I going to get dressed if I can't open my eyes?" Quinn demanded.

"Indie. Take care of this because I know she'll throw a hissy fit if I do it even though I don't want a piece of her. Much too high maintenance for me, even if I was straight."

"I'm right here and can hear you."

"I know," Sean said with an evil laugh.

"I'll help her. Come on, Quinn. I can't believe I'm doing this. I may need to shop for new friends," Indie grumbled and led Quinn to her bedroom.

"And miss all this fun and excitement?" Sean called after her. "I don't think so!"

Indie helped Quinn step into the dress and zipped her up. "Oh my goodness. Sean has really outdone himself this time. You look absolutely stunning."

"Can I open my eyes up yet?" Quinn asked.

"No!" Sean shouted from the living room. He scurried into the bedroom and tutted and fussed at the hemline and shoulders. Once he was satisfied, Sean told Quinn, "Now you can look."

Quinn blinked her eyes open and looked in the mirror. It didn't even look like her. She had cheekbones! And her eyes looked sexy. She turned and hugged Sean. "Thank you! Thank you! Thank you!"

Sean hugged her back and patted her on the butt, "Your welcome. Now go get yourself a man, sugar."

"Shoot. I look so good right now, I could probably get two boyfriends. I might have you come and fix my hair and makeup before every date."

"Oh no. Like I said, I love you, Quinnie, but you are much too high maintenance for me. Sean, pluck my eyebrows. Sean, blow dry my hair. Sean, fix me up with your cousin, Ricardo."

"Oh no you didn't!" Indie and Quinn both exclaimed at the same time.

"Hmmm…" Sean pursed his lips. "You know you want to run your fingers through his back hair."

"I threw up a little in my mouth." Quinn shivered in revulsion. "Yuck!"

"Get your shoes on. Zach's going to be here any minute to pick you up. Marty, Sean and I will be there in about a half an hour. Sean needs to finish getting ready." Indie shooed Quinn out of the bedroom.

"For Grandma Rose, I'm leaving Shawna at home and going to her party as the best-dressed

Mexican man she's ever laid eyes on."

"Grandma Rose would be okay with Shawna," Quinn said.

"I know, but I've decided it's okay to let Juan Carlos make an appearance sometimes, too."

Quinn heard a knock at the door and went to answer it.

"No! You go stand there in the lamplight. I'll answer the door," Sean said, as he pointed Quinn towards the middle of her living room.

Sean answered the door, and Zach walked in and stopped. "You take my breath away," he said to Quinn.

"Aw." Indie and Sean cooed in unison.

"Thank you," Quinn felt a momentary flush of shyness at all of the attention. She looked around for her evening bag. "You look pretty amazing yourself."

Zach wore a navy blue suit with a crisp white dress shirt and a dark blue silk tie. Quinn felt a small flutter in her stomach when she looked at him. "Are you ready to go?" He asked.

"I'm ready," Quinn said and took the elbow he offered. "I'll see you all at the restaurant."

Zach drove Quinn to Hanrahan's. They

didn't talk much on the short drive downtown. Zach had turned on a soft rock station. Quinn kept looking at Zach out of the corner of her eye. He really was handsome.

When they arrived at the restaurant, Quinn was quickly enveloped by a crowd of well-wishers there to celebrate Grandma Rose's birthday. Anne had gone to pick her mother up under the auspices of having a family dinner at Uncle Patrick's restaurant. Quinn looked around for Zach and saw he was engaged in conversation with her father. Her father laughed at something Zach said and slapped him on the back. Quinn started to make her way over towards them.

"They're here!" Someone called out. "Quick! Everybody quiet!"

Uncle Patrick dimmed the lights on the back side of the restaurant to help hide the party-goers. Quinn saw her mother help Grandma Rose down the sidewalk and through the front door.

"Surprise!" They all shouted.

Grandma Rose looked up, startled. "Oh my! Well, this is a surprise! Madelyn Wilbright, is that you? And George?" Grandma Rose was soon ensconced in the seat of honor at the head table as friends and family all surrounded her to wish her happy birthday.

Half an hour later, Quinn was chatting with a friend of her mother's when Uncle Patrick came up to her with a tall, older man in tow. "Quinn, I'd like you to meet Charlie Macomber. He's one of the instructors at your school. He's agreed to be your mentor chef."

"What are you talking about?" Anne Daniels said from behind Quinn. "What school? Mentor chef? Quinn, what's all this?" Anne's voice had grown shrill and everyone stopped to stare.

"I'm going to culinary school to be a chef," Quinn said in a small voice.

"What? A chef? Whatever for? You have a degree in journalism from a top school and you want to throw it away to cook for a living. I didn't sacrifice my life so my daughter could sling hash like a…"

Quinn stood white-faced and trembling. Zach made his way towards her, but when he grabbed her hand, she pushed him away.

"Anne, that's enough!" Rose Hanrahan commanded. "Enough! Into the kitchen this instant!" Rose grabbed her cane and moved her way towards the back of the restaurant. "Everyone continue with the party. We'll be back in five minutes. And you young man," Rose pointed her cane at Zach, "you stay put."

"Yes, ma'am," Zach said and took a seat at a nearby table.

Quinn, her parents and Uncle Patrick followed behind Grandma Rose. When the door to the kitchen swung shut, Anne turned on her brother and spat, "This is all your doing! I can't believe I let her come work for you. You've brainwashed my daughter into wanting to throw her life away to sweat in a kitchen!"

"Mother, I'm a grown woman, I made the decision, not Uncle Patrick."

"Well, you're not doing it. I forbid you to throw your entire future away on this!" She waved her hands and wrinkled her nose in distaste.

"Anne, that's enough," Quinn's father said quietly.

"I told you that your father and I could get you a job at the paper. You don't need to waste your life and your education. You had one bad experience for a no name Internet site. You'll bounce back," Anne continued.

"Anne, I said that is enough. Quinn is an adult. If she wants to be a chef, she can be a chef. Knowing her, she'll be the best damn chef this town has ever seen. No offense, Patrick," Quinn's father said.

"But she could work at a national newspaper. We know people." Anne protested and turned to Quinn. "Why in the world do you want to cook?"

"I want a family. I want to give my children something you never did. A home. Two parents that are home every day for their child, not chasing after some war lord in Africa. I want to make something with my hands, not spin stories to assuage whatever politico is in power."

"I never knew you felt this way," Anne said, shock on her face. "I thought you loved being with Grandma Rose. Ma, didn't she always beg to go to your house?"

"Anne, be quiet and listen, really listen to your daughter," Grandma Rose said.

"I love Grandma Rose." Quinn grabbed her grandmother's hand. "If not for her, I wouldn't have had nearly as wonderful childhood as I did. You, too, Uncle Pat." He nodded his head for her to continue. "But they didn't make up for not having you there. I wanted my mom and dad. You were too busy chasing stories, and when you were home, you were too busy trying to make me into something I'm not."

"I want you to have a better life than I did growing up," Anne said. "Honey, you don't know how hard it was when I was young."

"Yes, I do. Grandma and Uncle Patrick told me everything, but Mom, I'm not you. I'm never going to be you. I have to find my own way and sometimes I'm going to fail. It's okay. I love you, Mom, but I'm doing this. I'd like your blessing, but one way or another, I'm going to culinary school in January."

"Is it going to make you happy?" Anne asked, sniffling a little.

"Yes, Mom, it will. I love all of this. It makes me feel like…well, me."

"Fine. On one condition," Anne said.

"Anne, leave your daughter alone on this," Uncle Patrick said, warning filling his voice.

"Hold on, Patrick Hanrahan, and let me finish," Anne admonished. "Promise me if you do this that you'll be the best damned chef in the city."

Quinn hugged her mother. "I promise, Mom."

"And quit calling me Mother. I know you only do it when you're angry with me."

"Deal," Quinn said, laughing.

A cheer erupted from the dining room. "There's never a dull moment or lack of drama at an Irish party," Grandma Rose said, her eyes twinkling. "I'm proud of you, Quinn. You've given me the best birthday present ever. Now take me to meet your young man." Rose moved her way towards the dining room.

"He's not my young man," Quinn said. "He's my neighbor."

"Don't argue with your grandmother," Grandma Rose said. "I know when a man is smitten with a woman and a woman is smitten with a man. Stop fighting it."

"But…"Quinn protested. Her grandmother gave her a knowing look. "He is handsome."

"He has a good job and he's smart," Anne chimed in.

"I like him," Mr. Daniels said.

They walked into the dining room. Everyone acted like they hadn't all been listening at the door.

Sean and Indie rushed up to Quinn. "Are you okay? What happened? We came in after the big blow up and missed everything."

"I'm fine. Mom's fine. I'm going to culinary school. Where's Zach?" Quinn craned her neck and looked around the dining room. "Excuse me. I need to find my date."

"Oooh, girl, did you hear what she just said? She said date," Sean whispered loudly to Indie.

Quinn zigzagged her way through the tables until she stood in front of Zach. "Hi."

"Hi. Would you like something to drink?" He indicated the glass in front of him.

"In a minute. I've got something to say and I want to get it out before I lose my nerve. I like you," Quinn blurted. "I mean, I really like you and not in the friend way, but in the I want to wake up and have breakfast with you the next day kind of way."

"I…" Zach started.

"Hold on. I need to finish. I like you and I want to date you, but I'm a mess. I suck as a journalist. I got fired. I work part-time at a restaurant and am going back to school, so I'm all high maintenance and Sean says I can't even pluck my eyebrows right and you know what? I really want to kiss you right now."

"Are you finished?" Zach stood up.

Quinn waited for him to tell her she was crazy. Tears began to well in her eyes. "Yes," she said in a small voice.

"Good because I can't kiss you when you're talking." He pulled her to him and kissed her. Quinn's toes curled as a flutter and then an electric current raced through her veins. When he finally pulled away, he looked down at her. "I like you, too, Quinn Daniels. In fact, I'm half in love with you already."

"Does this mean I get to touch your telescope?" Quinn gave him a coy smile. She fluttered her lashes at him.

"Since this is our third date, I think that could be arranged."

"I like a man with a big telescope. All the better to see stars," Quinn whispered.

"Good to know," Zach whispered back and kissed her again.

EPILOGUE

http://theromancereport.blogathon.com

The Romance Report

A blog dedicated to the pursuit of love and happiness.

Monday, January 10, 8:37 a.m.

Well, dear readers, it's time for The Romance Report to close. It's been a journey and I thank you all for sticking by me as I learned a little bit about life and love and a whole lot about myself.

Lesson One: Nobody knows everything about life, but we should all pay closer attention to our grandparents and other older folks in our life. My Grandma and *Abuela* Reyna have given me more wisdom about life and love than I could have ever learned on my own.

Lesson Two: Romance is great, but love should be based on trust and friendship, too.

Lesson Three: Be yourself. If you do,

everything else falls into place.

That's all, dear readers. I have to get ready for school, and my boyfriend (I know! Exciting, isn't it!) is fixing me breakfast for my first day of school. Good luck in love, dear readers!

Comments:

Grayson 14: Does this mean you won't go to prom with me?

Dreambuilder: Sorry, dude. She's my girl now.

Quinn closed her laptop. "I'm nervous. What if I screw this up?"

"You won't screw this up," Zach said. He handed her a cup of coffee and a slice of toast with peanut butter. He kissed the top of her head. "I'm dating a future five star chef. You've got this. After all, you learned from Grandma Rose."

"You're right. I'd better get going if I'm going to make it to school on time."

"Good luck, sweetheart. I'll be here when you get home," Zach said.

"I don't need luck anymore. I already have everything I need right here." Quinn winked.

The End

Quinn's Smoky Mary Recipe

Ingredients

- 2 to 3 cups ice
- 1-2 limes, cut into wedges
- 1 tablespoon horseradish, drained
- 1 jalapeno pepper, quartered (more or less, depending on your desired level of heat)
- 2 teaspoons smoked salt (to taste in the drink and the rest for brimming)
- 2 cups vodka (more or less depending on the mood and how bad the date was)
- 3 cups spicy vegetable/tomato juice (the best organic juice with 1 tsp. ground chipotle pepper if you can find it)
- 1 tablespoon Worcestershire sauce
- Celery stalks for garnish
- Lemon and lime wedges for garnish

Directions

Muddle ice, lime wedges, horseradish, jalapeno, and salt in the bottom of a pitcher. Add vodka, tomato juice, and Worcestershire and stir to combine. Refrigerate if not serving immediately, or pour into glasses rimmed with chipotle pepper and smoked salt over ice. Garnish with celery stalk, and peppers. Enjoy and be sure to share with friends!

Preview

Permanently Deleted

Phee Jefferson Series

Coming December 2015

CHAPTER ONE

Phee sat at the circulation desk in the library. She was busy checking in the large cart of books next to her. She wanted to get everything done and shelved before she went home in a few minutes. The last patron was packing up to leave when Juliet burst through the front doors.

"Phee, you've got to come," Juliet panted.

"I'm busy, Juliet," Phee said. "I want to get this done."

Juliet slammed her hand down in front of Phee. Startled at her sister's sudden burst of anger, Phee looked up and saw Juliet was crying. "What in the world is the matter, Juls."

"It's Nellie Jo. They found Mike dead out at the pickle factory," Juliet sobbed, "and Clint's arrested Nellie Jo. Phee, he said she killed him. Nellie Jo killed her husband!"

Amy E. Lilly

Preview

Death Kicked the Milk Bucket

Coming Spring 2016

CHAPTER ONE

Claire stomped out of the building. Unfortunately, her attempt to slam the door failed miserably. It slowly eased shut and closed with a soft whoosh of air. The large overstuffed tote bag filled with ten years of her career slipped off her shoulder. Claire struggled to carry it all to her old Subaru parked in the company parking lot. As she yanked the tote bag back up, the strap ripped and everything tumbled to the pavement.

"Dang it! If one more bad thing happens, I swear I won't be responsible for my actions!" Claire declared to the empty lot. Sighing, she bent down to gather up her belongings. She heard a tearing sound as her pencil skirt split down the back. "Really? You have got to be kidding me. I guess that's what I get for challenging the universe." Claire finished gathering up her files and desk knickknacks and stuffed them back into her tote. She grabbed the tote around the bottom and made her way to her car. Claire fumbled around in her purse to find her keys and gave a triumphant "ha" when she yanked them from the detritus of her purse. As she popped open the trunk, Claire heard a tiny mew coming from the dumpster. As she slammed the trunk shut, another small meow sounded. Claire walked to the dumpster and peered inside. Nestled in a small cardboard box surrounded by garbage and rotting food was a tiny orange kitten. It looked up at her and let out another meow.

"Poor little thing. Are you hungry? Somebody must have dumped you here and left you to fend for yourself." Claire reached into the dumpster, lifted the fluffy orange kitten and snuggled him to her chest. It immediately started purring. "Well, you and I are just having a bad day. I got thrown out like trash, too. Would you like to come home with me?" As if it understood her, the kitten meowed and purred louder. Laughing, Claire picked carried the kitten to her car. She pulled a t-shirt from her gym bag, settled the furry bundle on to the passenger seat, then headed for her apartment.

Once home, Claire poured a small bowl of

milk for the kitten. "I guess you need a name. How about Gingersnap?" Claire sat down on the kitchen floor and gently stroked the kitten's back. "You can be Ginger for short." Claire's cellphone buzzed on the counter. She struggled up from the floor to answer. Isabella's name appeared on the screen and Claire hit the answer button.

"Hey, woman! How was your day?" Isabella asked cheerfully. In the background, Claire could hear the children laughing and yelling. "Knock it off you little monsters! I'm trying to talk to Claire and I can't hear over your screeching." After years of friendship, Claire was used to Isabella carrying on multiple conversations while on the phone.

"I got fired," Claire responded glumly.

"Oh my gosh, Claire! What happened?" Isabella asked in a shocked voice. "Kids, please be quiet! Go play in your room until dinner's ready. Matthew quit hitting your brother. Sorry, Claire. They're out of control with their dad out of town this week. So tell me everything."

"Nothing happened. Mr. Simpson called me into his office and started going on and on about the economic downturn and how sacrifices needed to be made...blah blah blah. Five minutes later, I am in HR signing papers. Before the ink was dry, a security guard told me that I had one hour to pack my desk and leave the building. Ten years on the job and I'm kicked to the curb like two-day old fish. It wasn't just me either. There were two other people let go today." Claire slumped onto her overstuffed couch, kicked off her heels and put her feet up on the coffee table.

"I am so sorry. What are you going to do?" Isabella asked.

"No clue. I don't even want to think about it tonight. I'll worry about it tomorrow. Darrin is supposed to take me out tonight. He called this morning and said he needed to see me. Maybe he's finally going to pop the question. He's been very secretive lately. I'm pretty sure he's been ring shopping. I'll be Mrs. Stanislowski. Wife of Dr. Stanislowski. Claire Stanislowski." Claire let the name roll off her lips. "It sounds kind of posh."

"If you say so." Isabella grunted. She was not a fan of Darrin. In her opinion, he was boring and uptight. "Well, I've got to get dinner ready before the kids eat the dog. Text me when you get home tonight."

"Will do. Bye." Claire disconnected and

pulled herself up from the couch. Darrin was going to be there to pick her up soon, so she needed to hurry and get ready. He hated to be kept waiting. She pulled off her now ruined skirt and kicked it next to her hamper. Slipping off her stockings and silk blouse, Claire rummaged around in her closet for something slinky and sophisticated to wear. She chose a deep turquoise dress with a scoop neck and slipped it over her head. She quickly pulled her hair into a French twist and freshened her makeup. She added a pair of tear drop silver earrings and slipped her feet into her favorite black peekaboo toe heels. As she was spritzing on perfume, a knock sounded on her door.

Claire hurried to the door to let Darrin in. "Hi, sweetheart. Right on time. I just need to grab my purse, and I'll be ready to go."

"Claire, I'd like to talk to you," Darrin walked in and shut the door behind him.

"Uh...okay? You sound serious. Let's go into the living room." Claire thought he must be nervous and wanted to ask her in private. Darrin wasn't a fan of public displays of affection. She sat down on the couch. Instead of sitting next to her, Darrin sat in the chair. "What did you want to talk about?" She gave him an encouraging smile.

"This isn't easy for me. We've been seeing each other for a while now." Darrin cleared his throat and swallowed. "And Claire, it's just...I've been seeing somebody else." He looked everywhere but at her.

Shocked, Claire struggled to grasp what he had just told her. "How long?"

"Does that really matter? I mean, what matters is that you and I aren't a good fit. You should just accept that it's over." Darrin finished stiffly. He started to stand up.

"No. No, I don't think so. You don't come in here and out of the blue tell me you've been seeing someone else and then walk out the door. I'm sorry, but I deserve an explanation. No. Scratch that. I demand an answer. We've been seeing each other for almost a year. I have gone to all of your boring functions. I've been nice to your mother which is no easy feat, let me tell you. That woman is a dragon from hell. I've smiled and schmoozed everyone you told me to schmooze even when they were busy grabbing my butt the minute your back was turned. So, you, Darrin Stanislowski, owe me a freakin' explanation!" Claire's voice had risen in volume.

She was so upset she was trembling.

"It's not you, Claire. You've been great. You are great. You and I together as a couple are not so great," Darrin said calmly. His lack of emotion angered Claire. She felt her ears get hot.

"Really? It's not me? How could it not be me? You are dumping me on what has already been a horrible day! I deserve an explanation!" Claire demanded angrily.

"I'm gay. Okay. Are you happy?" Darrin yelled back at her. His words immediately dampened her anger. "I'm tired of hiding who I am. I'm tired of using you to hide it. You deserve better. I knew you were expecting a marriage proposal soon. It's not like you've been subtle. I don't want to live a lie anymore. I'm planning on telling my friends and family, but I felt you deserved to hear it from me first. I'm sorry, Claire. I didn't mean to hurt you." Darrin's unhappiness filled the room.

"Wait. You're gay. Really?" Claire was trying to process what he had just told her. "Are you actually seeing someone or did you just say that to make it easier for me to hate you?" She was trying to wrap her brain around the idea of the man she had been seeing for the past year wasn't who she thought he was.

"I've met someone. He's made me realize that I don't have to live a lie. You would like him, Claire. He's funny and smart. He makes me happy. I want someone to make you happy like that, too." He gave her a sad smile. "I am so sorry that I've been lying to you. I hope you'll forgive me and we can be friends."

"I just...I don't know. I mean, I'm just not understanding how I didn't realize. Listen, can you just go now? I want to be by myself. I need to be alone. So please, just go." Claire wiped the angry tears that had started to fall with the back of her hand.

"I understand. Claire, I really am sorry." Darrin tried to give her a hug, but Claire shrugged him off. He walked out of the apartment and shut the door quietly behind him.

Once he was gone, Claire sat back down on the sofa and leaned her head back as she tried to accept what she just heard. Her boyfriend of a year had just dumped her for a guy. She got laid off from the only job she had ever held. She had less than a month's worth of savings in the bank and a fifteen-year-old Subaru that was a crap shoot every day on whether it would start. Claire felt a tickle on her cheek. She turned her head to see Ginger sniffing her. She reached up and stroked the kitten's fuzzy head. "Well, Ginger, looks like we've only got each other, girl. What are we going to do?" Ginger leaped down on to Claire's lap and curled up to go to sleep. "You've got exactly the right idea, girl." Claire kicked off her shoes and settled back onto the couch to figure out her next move.

Claire awoke to kitten whiskers tickling her chin. She gave Gingersnap a quick pat on the head and put her on the ground. A quick glance at the clock and Claire realized she had slept through the night. It was early morning and the sun was just peeking up over the city's skyline. She went into her small kitchen and started a pot of coffee. She popped a bagel in the toaster and searched through her fridge for cream cheese. Her refrigerator shelves revealed a limp bunch of carrots next to a jar of olives but nothing else. She settled on strawberry jam. Smearing the bagel with a large dollop of jam and pouring a cup of coffee, Claire sat on the bar stool at her kitchen counter. She opened her laptop and began to search the online help wanted ads. "Hmmmm...let's see if we can find someplace looking for an out-of-work history major whose only experience is writing advertisements for a pharmaceutical company." Claire tapped away at the keyboard. "Let's see...secretary wanted. Must type 80 words per minute. That leaves me out." Claire spent the next hour browsing through job after job. She glumly realized she wasn't qualified for most positions in the history field. She had dropped out of her Master's program halfway through her second year when she landed the position at Gaston Pharmaceuticals thanks to a referral from an ex-boyfriend who used to work there. The money had been good and she had jumped at the opportunity. Now, she found herself with no job, a useless degree and no prospects. She closed her laptop and decided to call her mom.

"Hi, Mom! It's me, Claire," Claire said with a false cheerfulness.

"You're up bright and early on a Saturday. What's wrong?" Claire's mother, Mary, had a sixth sense when it came to her children.

"Well, let's see. I got laid off, found a kitten, and Darrin dumped me for a guy," Claire declared in a matter-of-fact tone. "Other than that, I'm good. And you?"

"Gracious! I didn't expect all of that. Let's back up. Start with losing your job," Mary said. Claire proceeded to tell her mother all that transpired the day before. When she finished, her mom was silent on the other end of the line.

"Mom, are you still there?" Claire asked.

"Sorry, dear. I was just thinking about what you said. The funniest thing happened the other day, and I haven't had a chance to talk to you about it. I received a letter from the law firm handling your Great Aunt Lily's estate. It's finally been settled and well, everything has been left to me. It's not much, but she left her farm and a small yearly allowance to operate it with the stipulation that it stay in the family. I would venture to say that you have no savings and now that Darrin is out of the picture, nothing to keep you in the city."

"I wouldn't say nothing. I have friends and a life and..." Claire trailed off as it dawned on her what her mother was suggesting. "Mom, are you suggesting I move to Aunt Lily's farm? In the country? With cows and things?"

"Why not? The house and farm needed to be sorted out and you could go for the short term while you figure out what you want to do.

Expensive shoes and a nice wardrobe can only carry you so far in life. They certainly aren't going to pay your electric bill. Plus, you'd be helping me out. I don't have time to go up there to go through the house until the end of the school year. This is a win-win for you and me," Mary said emphatically. Claire's mother was an elementary school teacher, and she was used to having her directions followed. "Your father can't do it with his busy practice. Your sister is up to her eyeballs in wedding plans and your brother won't be back from Africa for at least three months. It makes sense."

"Let me think about it. I mean, everything just happened to me yesterday. I haven't even had time to sort it out in my brain or see if I can even get another job. Besides, the only time I've been to the country is the one time we visited Aunt Lily. I got stung by a bee and swelled up like a puffer fish. It wasn't exactly a good experience. Cows and chickens don't really hold any appeal for me." Claire shook her head at her mom's suggestion. Claire living in the country in her Ferragamo boots. It just wouldn't work.

"Well, don't think about it too long. Someone needs to head up and get the keys from the attorney's office and make sure the house is still standing. It's my understanding that a neighbor has been taking care of all of the animals and checking on the house. He's been kind enough to do it for the past two months, but I am sure he doesn't want to continue indefinitely. You could consider it a retreat. A chance to rethink the direction of your life. Regroup." Claire's father was a psychologist and unfortunately, his psychobabble worked his way into his wife's vocabulary.

"Give me a few days. I'll talk to you later, Mom. Love you," Claire said as she disconnected the call. Claire couldn't even wrap her brain around the idea of heading to the country. She was a city girl through and through. She loved the sounds and smells of the city streets. The bright lights and crowds were part of her. She couldn't even imagine not being able to get to a Starbucks in less than a few blocks.

Claire decided she needed a second opinion. She picked up her cell phone to call Isabella. "Isabella's House of Chaos. How can I be driven insane today?" Isabella answered. "Claire, I swear if these kids don't settle down I am going to lose my mind. We definitely need a spa day."

"Good morning to you, too. So, I'm not going to be Mrs. Stanislowski. In fact, no one will be Mrs. Stanislowski. It will end up being Dr. Darrin Stanislowski and Mr. Stanislowski," Claire gave a grimace as the image of Darrin slipping a diamond ring on another man's hairy knuckles formed in her mind.

"I don't get it. What the heck are you talking about?" Isabella demanded.

"Darrin needed to talk to me last night. He has decided to come out of the closet. I was the first person he came out to by dumping me for a guy. So I lost my job and my boyfriend to another man all in one day. This is what I get for cursing the universe. And now my mom wants me to go live on my Great Aunt Lily's farm and sort out her estate."

"Crap on a cracker! I knew something was off about that guy, but even I didn't see that one coming! I would love to have been a fly on the wall to see that meltdown. How badly did you hurt him?" Isabella asked.

"I didn't even raise my voice," Claire protested. "Well, okay, I did yell just a little, but can you blame me? I did not see this coming at all. I was a gay man's beard. I am a clueless idiot."

"You and the rest of us. Claire, I just thought he was uptight. I would never have guessed Darrin was gay. And your mom is crazy if she thinks you would survive in the country. She obviously didn't see you freak out when a pigeon came too close to you at the park. I thought you were going to hyperventilate and pass out from fear. A chicken would make you have a stroke," Isabella chuckled.

"I just don't like pigeons. They are dirty birds. I could survive in the country if I had to. I just prefer the city. I haven't even had a day to look for a job. I'm sure I'll find something. If need be, I'll swing up to Cosner's Creek to make sure the farm is still standing then head back home," Claire said. She poured herself another cup of coffee and stirred the last bit of sugar she scraped from the sugar bowl. She would have to head to the store this morning to get groceries and some kitten food for Gingersnap.

"If you say so. Don't do anything rash. You've had a crappy twenty-four hours. I know you, chica, and you are going to do something crazy that you'll regret later. As your friend, I am telling you now - don't do it," Isabella warned.

"I'm not going to do anything crazy. Right

now, I am going to head to the store. My kitten needs some food. Call me later," Claire said.

"Will do. Come by later today and I'll feed you. I'm making *chile rellenos* and flan just for you. Comfort food is a must in these trying times. Talk to you later." Isabella hung up. She knew the way to Claire's heart was through her cooking especially since Claire didn't cook. She microwaved. She tossed salads and occasionally made pasta but that was the extent of her kitchen skills.

Claire hopped in the shower. Once she toweled dry, she pulled on a sweatshirt she dug out of her messy dresser. She yanked a pair of yoga pants and socks out of her gym bag, sniffed them and deciding they could last at least another day, pulled them on. She put laundry on her to-do list for the day. Grabbing her keys, she walked down to the street and hopped into her Subaru. She turned the key and the engine roared to life. She put it into drive and as she pulled out, the car gave a horrible clunk, the check engine light came on, and it shuddered to a stop. Claire tried to start it again and nothing happened. Claire climbed out of the car and called the garage that did her oil changes and tune-ups. Twenty minutes later, a tow truck pulled up and Iggy hopped out. His dad owned the garage, but Iggy had taken over the day-to-day operations a year ago after his dad's heart attack.

"What's up, Miss O'Connor? Car won't start?" Iggy chomped away at a piece of gum. His greasy black hair was styled into unbecoming spikes which gave him the look of a slightly crazed hedgehog. His face was pock-marked, and he had an unfortunately large beaked nose. His arms were covered with tattoos. If Claire hadn't known him for years, she would have crossed the street to avoid him, but he was actually a decent guy.

"I started to pull out and it gave a loud kerplunk. Then it died and wouldn't start back up," Claire shrugged her shoulders. "I don't know what's wrong with her." She handed Iggy her keys. He slid into the driver's seat and tried to start the car. Nothing happened. He hopped out and opened the hood. He fiddled with some wires and gave an occasional grunt. "How bad is it?"

"Well, it ain't good. I'm going to have to tow her to the shop. It looks like the timing belt and that is bad. It could be the death of this old girl." Iggy patted the hood of the car like it was an old horse.

"I can't afford a new car!" Claire wailed.

"Heck, I can't afford this car if it's an expensive repair!"

"I'll see what I can do. I can't make you any promises. I'll call you later today and tell you the damage," Iggy said. "I won't charge you for the tow. It's just down the block anyway."

"Thanks, Iggy. Just do your best." Claire's shoulders slumped as she realized that her bad luck wasn't over. She headed down the street to walk to the market. It was only five blocks and the walk would clear her head. Obviously, someone was trying to tell her something. She had no job, no man, no money and now, no car. Her grandma said bad luck came in threes, so she was due some good luck. Maybe she should buy a lottery ticket. She kicked at a soda can in the middle of the sidewalk.

"Ma'am, there's no littering," A voice said from behind her. Startled, Claire turned and saw a policeman. He pulled out a book and a pen from his back pocket. "I'm going to have to write you a ticket."

"But...but...I...oh, never mind." Claire gave a dejected sigh and gave him her name and address. She snatched the ticket from his hand the second he reached out to hand it to her.

Claire walked the remaining few blocks to the market, picked up some kitten food and a few other essentials and headed home. When she opened her apartment door, Gingersnap ran up to greet her. "You know what, Ginger? I think the universe has been beating me over the head the past two days and telling me it is time to make a change. How about you and I take a little trip to the country?" Ginger meowed her agreement.

Claire turned her car turned down the lane marked with a large wooden sign that read "Lilly Belle Farm." She had used the last of her savings to repair her car. Isabella had helped her pack her apartment and Claire's dad had hauled all of her furniture and dishes to a storage unit. Claire had brought her laptop, her clothes and a cat carrier with Ginger inside to Aunt Lily's farm. She wasn't planning on staying for more than two or three months, so she figured she wouldn't need too many things. She was doing what her mom suggested. Reevaluating her life and deciding what direction to go with her defunct career. She hadn't really liked writing ads. Her true passion was American history. Claire thought about returning to grad school and finishing her thesis. She could teach history at a local community college or get a job at a museum. Her mind was wandering and she wasn't paying attention to the road in front of her. It wasn't until she heard a loud honk did she startle out of her reverie and realize that she had stopped her car. An old truck was behind her waiting for her to move. Pressing on the gas, Claire continued up the lane until she spotted Aunt Lily's farmhouse. It was much larger than she remembered. Pulling up to the house, she parked and stepped out to stretch her legs after the long drive. The driver of the old truck followed her into the driveway and pulled to a stop behind her car. A tall man stepped out and walked towards her.

"Can I help you?" The man asked as he squinted at Claire from under the brim of his battered cowboy hat. He wore a dusty pair of jeans with beat-up cowboy boots and his blue t-shirt stretched across his broad chest. Claire couldn't really see his face since it was hidden by the hat, but she didn't like the proprietary tone he took with her. This was her family's home and she had no clue who he was.

"I don't know. Can you?" Claire responded saucily. "This is my Great Aunt Lily's house. Well, it was her house. It's my mom's now. I'm Claire O'Connor. So the question is, who are you and how can I help you?"

"Whoa. A little prickly, aren't you. I'm Wade Daniels. I've been taking care of your aunt's place since she passed away. I live right down the road at Hidden Acres Farm. I saw a strange car pulling up here and figured I'd better check it out. We don't get much crime in Cosner's Corner, but you never be too careful." Wade took off the cowboy hat and Claire could see he had the brightest blue eyes she had ever seen. In fact, he was absolutely gorgeous. Curly black hair with tanned skin and a hint of an afternoon shadow on his chin. The chin even had a small cleft in the middle. He could have stepped out of GQ magazine. Claire gulped. Country life was already making her feel better.

"Sorry. I just drove four hours, got lost twice and haven't eaten since dawn. I'm a little on edge," Claire patted at her ponytail tucking the stray pieces behind her ear. She probably looked like a second-hand store reject after driving in the car with the windows rolled down. "It's nice to meet you. I appreciate you taking care of the farm until one of us could come up here."

"Not a problem. Did you already pick up keys to the place? The attorney said someone was coming up this week, so I put some milk in the fridge and there's a loaf of homemade bread in the breadbox. I cleaned out the refrigerator when Rose died, but the pantry is fully stocked with canned goods from last summer. You might need to light the stove though. It's kind of touchy, so if you'd like I can show you how to do it," Wade offered.

"That would be great. I'm not much of a cook, so I'll probably just microwave something. Let me get my kitten out of the car." Claire reached in the car and grabbed Gingersnap's carrier out.

"You won't be microwaving anything. This house hasn't been updated very much since the 1920's. It still has the old knob and tube wiring in place. There is no way a microwave would work in this old house. Haven't you ever been here before?" Wade grabbed the carrier from Claire as she fumbled with the set of keys the attorney had given her.

"I came here once as a child. My mom would come by herself to visit Aunt Lily. She said it was her break from her children to come to the country." Claire finally got the key to turn in the lock of the front door and it swung inward. "I'm not much of a country person. I've lived in the city my entire life. I had a chance to help my mom out by coming up here for a few months, so here I am." She walked into the front entry of the house. Claire saw the floors were wide oak plank floors that were worn but had a warm glow from years of waxing. There was a large sitting room off to the left. Claire took the cat carrier from Wade and set it on the floor. When she opened the latch, a bright orange ball of fluff streaked out of the cage and darted under an armchair in the corner. Green eyes glared up at Claire. "Somebody's not happy riding in a car."

"Cute kitten. Your aunt had a cat. I took her back to my house since it didn't seem right to leave her here alone. Her name is Cream. She takes off and heads back here every chance she can slip out of the door. If you don't mind, I'll bring her back here later today. Here, let me show you where everything is." Wade walked out of the sitting room and back into the hallway. There was a stairway to the upstairs to the right of the front door, but Wade headed down the hallway. The hall opened up into a large dining room with a large oak table with four sturdy chairs around it. Heavy drapes hung over the windows shutting out the spring sun. Claire decided that she would have to let some light into the dark rooms. She had noticed that the sitting room had heavy drapes as well. Off of the dining room was a large country kitchen. The cupboards had glass fronts and Claire spotted an eclectic mix of dishes. The counters were made of marble and wood which surprised Claire.

"The counters are beautiful! Is that really marble?" Claire trailed her fingers across the top of the cool surface.

"Yes. It's called a breadboard. This house was built in the twenties and was pretty modern for the time from what Rose said. The cook that used to live here with your aunt when she was young used to make pies and breads on that marble top. You're lucky that your aunt at least modernized the stove from coal to gas within the past fifty years. The old stove is out on the summer porch and Rose still used it for canning in the summer."

"I guess I'm going to have to learn to cook since I guess take-out isn't really an option around here," Claire joked. Her gaze took in the old refrigerator that looked like it had been here since the 1950's. A large sink with a hand pump caught her eye and she suddenly had a sinking thought. "Please tell me I have running water and an inside bathroom."

Wade laughed. "You do. There is a small bathroom right behind that door over there and there is a full bathroom upstairs. The house has been updated some, but it still needs some work to bring it into the modern age."

"Well, I guess using my laptop is out of the question," Claire gave Wade a wry smile. "I was going to try to update my resume and do some job hunting while I was up here, but that seems like it might be out of the question."

"You'll have to go to the coffee shop in Cosner's Corner if you want internet or to the local library. No wi-fi here. The goats don't really need it." Wade opened up a door on the right side of the kitchen. "You've got a fully stocked pantry and this other door is the back stairway." He closed the pantry door and opened the door next to it. A set of stairs led upstairs.

Claire headed up the narrow stairs conscious of Wade walking behind her. She was glad she had worn her Lucky jeans which gave her butt an extra boost. She came to the top of the stairs which opened to a large landing. Turning she walked down the hall and opened the first door to her left. Inside was a small, but neat bedroom with a single bed covered by a cheerful quilt. The next door opened up to a linen closet filled with sheets, towels and quilts. Claire opened the final door on the left and found what must have been her aunt's bedroom. A large bed was covered with a quilt made of varying shades of blue fabric. There was a large wooden wardrobe in the corner, a rocking chair and a bright rag rug on the wooden floor. Claire saw a faded pair of pink house slippers under the bed. It made her sad that she hadn't known her Great Aunt Lily. Claire and her sister Catherine preferred to visit the father's family who lived near the beach. Great Aunt Lily seemed eccentric living in her old farmhouse with her farm animals. Now Claire would never know what she was like and she realized a piece of her family's history had been lost with the death of her aunt.

Claire opened a door at the end of the hallway. It revealed a small bathroom with a large claw foot tub, a pedestal sink and thank goodness, a toilet. She noticed that there was no shower. Claire thought she might like sitting in the deep tub filled with bubbles. It really could be like a spa retreat.

"You'll like this next room," Wade said as he led Claire back into the hallway. He opened the door on the right side of the hallway. Claire stepped into a room with a large window with a deep window seat perfect for sitting and reading a book. The room was painted a pale blue. There was a double bed on a white metal frame. A beautiful quilt of navy blue with applique stars covered the bed and a large handmade rug made from denim covered most of the hardwood floor. A bookcase stood against one wall and was filled with old books. A small white dresser sat in the corner.

"I love it. I'll move my things in here," Claire said decisively. She whirled around taking in the bright spring sunlight as it reached across the room. For the first time in a month, Claire felt a little glimmer of hope that her luck had changed. Maybe this country retreat would do her some good.

Wade and Claire headed back downstairs using the front stairway. Gingersnap had ventured out from her hiding spot and was sniffing the doors and furniture. "Let me go ahead and light the stove for you," Wade offered as he headed back towards the kitchen. As he worked on the stove, Claire opened the door off the back of the kitchen. She stepped out onto a large enclosed porch with a hammock and two rocking chairs. On the other end of the porch was the old coal stove with stacks of canning jars next to it. There were several pairs of boots lined up by the door. Claire gazed out into the backyard and spotted the large white barn surrounded by grassy fields.

"I've got the stove lit for you. It's time to feed the animals. You should come with me so you can see what to do." Wade opened the screen door and headed towards the barn.

Reluctantly, Claire followed behind him. She had forgotten there were animals involved. She steeled her resolve. She could do this. How hard could it be? Throw some food in a bowl and give them water. Piece of cake. "I've got this," Claire told herself. She stepped into the barn behind Wade and the smell threatened to overwhelm her. "Oh! What is that horrible smell?" Claire gagged.

Wade laughed. "It's just Banjo. He's the male buck visiting Rose's does for the month. Rose had arranged for Joe Boxley to bring Banjo whenever Morning Dawn went into heat. I figured you would want to keep the same breeding schedule that Rose had, so I went ahead and brought Banjo over."

"Buck? Doe? Heat? What the heck are you talking about?" Claire started to realize that she might be in over her head. "I thought Aunt Lily had a couple of cows and chickens and now you're talking about deer?"

"Deer?" Wade let out a loud bark of laughter. "No, not deer. Come here and look." Wade motioned for Claire to come look in the large pen at one side of the barn. She peered through the darkness to see a large white goat with long horns and a beard staring balefully at her. He stuck his nose into a hay feeder on the wall and pulled out a piece of hay and slowly chewed it. The musky odor was stronger near his pen.

"He needs a bath. He really stinks!" Claire shook her head.

"That's because male goats pee on their face to attract the females," Wade told Claire with a smile. He leaned through the fence and patted the goat on his side.

"Now you are just yanking my chain. Really?" Claire gave him a look of disbelief. "If any guy I was interested in did that, I would run screaming in the other direction."

"I'm not kidding. We'll need to let him out into the pen with Morning Dawn tomorrow, but for now he can stay put. Come and meet the girls. We need to give them fresh hay and water. You give them grain in the morning, but not too much. They'll get fat." Wade led her out of the back of the barn and into the fenced field behind it. As they came back into the sunlight, a herd of white goats looked up from where they were nibbling on brush, then started trotting towards them. Claire let out a small scream of fright and hid behind Wade. "These are the does. They won't hurt you. The only thing they might do is nibble on your clothes."

Claire stepped out from behind Wade and timidly held out her hand to the goat closest to her. It leaned forward and nibbled on her fingers. Claire felt a little braver and she patted the goat on its head. "Nice goat. Pretty goat. Goat that doesn't want to eat me." Claire said in an effort to make friends. No sooner had she petted the one goat when others were butting their heads against her leg and vying for attention. "Whoa! One at a time!"

"They're hungry. Come here and I'll show

you what to do." Wade led her to a small door on one side of the door. Inside were bags with goat and chicken feed and buckets. Wade showed her how much to feed them and how to fill the hay feeders. He showed her how much chicken feed to toss around the yard in the morning and afternoon and how to water all of them. Afterwards, Claire thought that it was definitely something she could handle.

"This isn't nearly as bad as I thought it would be," Claire said cheerfully to Wade.

"Don't get too ahead of yourself. I'll be back in the morning at six a.m. to show you how to milk the does that need it and then once a week you have to muck out the barn," Wade instructed her.

"Milk? As in, milk coming from goats?" Claire gave Wade an incredulous look. "Mucking?"

"You see that building over there?" Wade pointed to a small building that Claire hadn't noticed before. A small stone path led between it and the house. "That is the milking shed and cheese house. Your aunt made goat cheese and sold it to the local restaurants in the area. She also sold it with her organic vegetables at the farmer's market in town on Saturday mornings. I assumed that whoever took over the farm was going to continue with the cheese and gardening."

"I don't know anything about cheese except that it tastes really good on a sandwich and I definitely don't know anything about gardening. What was my mother was thinking sending me up here to take care of this place? I should just get Gingersnap and head home." Claire gave a defected kick to the dirt in front of her. She noticed her designer boots had mud and muck from the barnyard on them. Great.

ABOUT THE AUTHOR

Amy Lilly grew up in the small town of Cedaredge, Colorado where she spent her free time reading Nancy Drew mysteries and using her Junior Detective Kit to solve mysteries on her family farm. Amy earned a B.A. in English from the University of Iowa and her M.L.S. from SUNY at Buffalo. She spends her free time raising goats, chickens, a herd of well-fed cats and two hyperactive Jack Russell Terriers. She is married with two sons and two beautiful, smart granddaughters.

www.ingramcontent.com/pod-product-compliance
Lightning Source LLC
Chambersburg PA
CBHW030808310726
48980CB00006B/424/J

* 9 7 8 0 6 9 2 5 1 5 4 5 7 *